THE LONG, BIG KISS GOODBYE

THE LONG, BIG KISS GOODBYE
Scott Montgomery

First published in England in 2007 by
Telos Publishing Ltd
61 Elgar Avenue, Tolworth, Surrey, KT5 9JP, England
www.telos.co.uk

Telos Publishing Ltd values feedback. Please e-mail us with any
comments you may have about this book to:
feedback@telos.co.uk

ISBN: 978-1-84583-109-7
The Long, Big Kiss Goodbye © Scott Montgomery 2007

Printed and bound in Great Britain by Biddles Ltd., King's Lynn

1 2 3 4 5 6 7 8 9 10 11 12 13 14 15

British Library Cataloguing in Publication Data.
A catalogue record for this book is available from the British
Library.

For Mum and Dad.

Chapter One

Nice guys finish dead

Wanna know why New York's called the Big Apple? 'Cos it's rotten to the core. On a good day, you'd bite into it and find half a maggot.

On a bad day?

My office was so far Downtown my clients had to hail a cab from Hell just to get there. And they always kept the meter running. The place was crummier than a sponge cake that had been put through a mincer; but it had character. Last week, the Department of Health said it had so much more than that. I'm thinking of asking the rats for their share of the rent.

Betty's tiny reception area was out front, with another door leading to my minuscule private office. I had given her the day off, since there was nothing for her to do. She was a good girl, and an even better secretary. But I didn't employ her for her typing skills.

The room was little more than a shoebox with a filing cabinet. The battleship-grey paint was flaking from the walls. Cheap, dime store paintings hung there at angles more crooked than the bigwigs down at the DA's office. It was damp. The carpet was frayed, and, apart from the hat stand in the corner, I only had space for one other chair. Told you it had character.

Lola's strip joint was across the street. The steady flicker of the neon sign blinked through the slats in the Venetian blinds, illuminating my place like a metronome of throbbing, garish pink light.

If this was the asphalt jungle, then I could hear the sounds of all the animals that wore a human disguise. I could make out the noise of various species viciously defending their territory; knuckle-dragging primates beating their chests in triumph; the howl of police sirens echoing in the night; and the hopeful mating calls of drunk guys falling for unattainable girls, before being bounced out onto the hard, unloving concrete of the pavement. They soon fell for the not-quite-as-appealing allure of the gutter.

The detective business was like a faulty cannon. Not exactly booming. You could say that things were slow. Slower than a soused snail that had been stamped into the sidewalk. You could say that. But it wouldn't make any sense.

I was wearing a navy blue suit, a fresh, white cotton shirt, spotted tie and matching handkerchief. I was flat broke, but at least I did it in style. I leaned back in my swivel chair and swung my feet up onto the desk. My polished, size 12 brogues shone in the intermittent moonlight. I struck a match on the side of the desk and lit a cigarette. I was trying to quit, so now I only smoked after dinner. The local quack thinks I oughta give up eating instead.

I put out the match. Its sulphurous stink mingled with the smell of damp, successfully creating a whole new aroma. I used to be a flat foot. Now I was a down-at-heel gumshoe. Coupla years ago, I pounded the beat every night, but, on one particular gig, my timing was lousy. Makes me sound like a cross between a good cop and a bad drummer. But that's another story. Remind me to tell you sometime.

And then there was the door. That's where She came in.

In my experience, dames are like coffee. They start off hot, sweet and fulla beans. But they quickly turn cold and bitter, and leave a bad taste in your mouth. Yup, if women are caffeine-based beverages, then I'm a mug every time. That's a whole load of other stories. Maybe I should open a library.

Let's get back to *this* dame. She was so like a girlie magazine centrefold come to life: I wondered if she had staples on her belly. She wasn't a blonde bombshell; more like a war zone. Dressed to kill, and with a body to die for. Appropriately enough, get involved with a doll like this, and you usually wind up on a slab in the morgue. Or worse. Married.

The broad's clothes clung to those curves like a koala bear hugging a eucalyptus tree. Her angora sweater resembled two watermelons doing the fandango under a pink carpet. The lower half of her body was encased in a black skirt that stuck to her like it could've been made of liquorice. The hemline was above the knee – both of them. I studied her heart-shaped face as intently as a freshman attending his first college lecture. She had eyes of blue that were deeper than the Atlantic Ocean. Long lashes fluttered above them like exotic butterflies. The brows above those were slender and dark. Her button nose was small but perfectly formed. Her cheekbones were so striking they could've been designed by an architect. Her red lips drooped mischievously, like ripe cherries on stalks.

'Sharp?' she said, exposing white teeth as perfect as polished porcelain. 'Jack Sharp?'

'That's me,' I replied. 'Who might you be?' A blue-grey haze of cigarette smoke hung in the air like fumes from a car exhaust pipe. She ignored my question. I dunno why. It was a perfectly good one. Polite too.

She cooed: 'I need a private eye with his ear to the ground, and I hear you're a dick with a heart.'

That statement had more body parts than a Bronx murder scene, but what did a dumb shmoe like me know? My education had consisted of being expelled from the School of Hard Knocks and flunking out of the University of Life.

'Yeah, well, hearts are like rules,' I drawled. 'Made to be broken.'

Whoever tipped her off about me knew fine well that I always had a soft spot for a dame in distress. The dame changed frequently over the years. But I never did.

She slinked over and perched herself on the side of my desk. My in-tray had just got a damn sight fuller. Normally, I didn't much care for paperwork, but I was keen to get her particulars down there and then. I knew that I needed this case. That was strictly on a need-to-know basis, and right about then, she didn't need to know that.

'I'm Kitty,' she purred, through those luscious, pouting lips. 'But you can call me Mrs O'Malley. You don't strike me as the sort of man who would follow the rules, Mr Sharp.'

I nodded. 'You got that right. Some people say I got a bad attitude. They can get lost.'

'Aren't you going to offer me a drink?'

She was so fulla feline grace, I almost poured her a saucer of milk.

She leaned forward, showing off an exquisite expanse of cleavage. I tried not to stare. But I didn't try very hard.

I could almost taste the tantalising, musky scent of her perfume. It was no cheap fragrance. Definitely something top-of-the-range from one of the pricier department stores. That meant she had money. She let out a cool, lingering breath that drifted towards me from her gorgeous, pursed lips like she was blowing me a deadly kiss. 'It's warm in here.' She smiled then, making a point of putting her right index finger in her mouth, gently, absent-mindedly biting at it with her small, pearly teeth.

Cute. Bad Kitty. Just the kinda pussy you might like sitting in your lap on a wet Sunday afternoon. I'd have wagered her bark was worse than her bite. But, then again, I wasn't a betting man. And I think I was getting my species mixed up.

'I'd offer you a cup of tea, Kitty. But I'm all outta tea. And cups.'

She didn't like that. 'I wanted something stronger anyway,' she hissed. 'And I always get what I want.' That pretty face suddenly hardened faster than quick-drying cement. In an instant, the coy smile became a grimace.

'Sure you do,' I replied. 'Mrs O'Malley, much as I'd love to hang around all night and admire your great ... wits,' I licked my lips, 'I got work ta do, so –'

'Yeah, looks like you've got a whole pack of cigarettes to smoke,' she interrupted. She reached for the pack, helped herself to a cigarette, lit it, and settled back on the desk. She crossed her legs, showing more thigh than was strictly necessary. She had decent thighs, indecently wrapped in sheer, black silk stockings that left little to the imagination. As far as I was concerned, imagination was overrated. 'Why don't you let me help you?' she asked, before taking a long draw on her cigarette. She exhaled a plume of smoke and balanced her feet on the vacant seat opposite my desk. She wore black stilettos that showed off her ankles.

I stubbed out the remains of my own cigarette in the overflowing ashtray and reached into the bottom drawer of my desk. I retrieved the liquor bottle and a grimy glass, and pushed the drawer shut with a slam. I filled the glass with dark, wood-coloured bourbon and handed it to her. She motioned upwards with her drink. I clinked the bottle against it. 'Bottoms up,' I said.

'To your very rude health.' The beginnings of a grin spread across her lips. I watched her raise the glass to her mouth. She took a sip, and swallowed, leaving a scarlet lipstick smear on the glass. The grin soured like a quart of milk that had been left in a Turkish bathhouse overnight. I could tell that the acrid taste burned her throat, but she didn't want it to show.

I took a long slug from the bottle, swirling the contents around my mouth before wolfing them down in one gulp. It was like gargling neat paint stripper with a twist of lemon. I wanted to light another cigarette, but was afraid my head might explode. I put the bottle back in the drawer.

'Let's get down to business, Jack,' she said. 'Can I call you Jack?'

'Lady, you can call me anything you want – including Gwyneth – just as long as I get 30 bucks a day. Plus expenses.'

Her eyes narrowed like a couple of dark slits cut in paper. 'You some kind of comedian now? Because that's the funniest thing I've heard all day.'

I sneered. 'My material don't come cheap.'

'Neither do you, it seems,' she said through clenched teeth. 'Twenty-five. Take it or leave it.'

'Guess I'll leave it,' I bluffed.

'What, you think I'm some kind of dumb blonde?' she retaliated, all defensive-like. Her forehead crinkled slightly just above her nose. She looked even more attractive when she was angry.

'Right about now, I don't even think you're a blonde.'

'Go to hell.'

'Ladies first.'

Her shoulders slumped slightly, and she gave an exasperated sigh.

I get that a lot.

'Are you always this stubborn?' she asked.

'Always.'

'Thirty dollars a day,' she said, sheepishly. 'Plus expenses.'

Round one to me.

I settled back in my chair once more. She knew that this was her cue to talk. She had a story to tell and the audience was sitting comfortably. When you become a private investigator, you witness the seamy side of life. And New York City was seamier than a warehouse fulla bust sofas. You witness the lies, the pain, the jealousy, the torment, the anguish, the cruelty and the heartbreak. Hell, you don't just witness it. You cause some of it. It's all part of the job. Sometimes I love to hate this dirty, nasty job. Sometimes I hate to love it. But I'm too old to run away to the circus. The only good thing is what you learn about human nature and human behaviour. Kitty was desperate, and at her wits' end. Or she'd have walked straight out the door just as assuredly as she'd walked through it. And when it came to dames, I'd seen it all, done it all and heard it all.

'I want you to kill me, Jack.'

Right. Even I had to admit I hadn't heard that one before.

Chapter Two

A deal to die

Round two to Kitty.

If we'd actually been in the ring, then she'd have just caught me with a sharp right uppercut, straight under the chin when my guard was down. My punch-drunk mind was on the ropes, wandering, trying to figure what her angle was. 'Murder's illegal in this town,' I said, playing for time, trying to appear unfazed. 'Not that it stops anyone.'

Kitty took a sip from her glass. She was used to the taste of the bourbon by now. 'Will I be paying for you to state the obvious, or is it just a natural talent of yours?'

'All part of the service,' I replied. 'Now, you gonna tell me what this is all about?'

Her face was cold. She took a breath. Then looked me straight in the eyes. 'I want you to help me fake my death. I need to disappear.'

'The sign on the door says "Private Investigator", lady. I ain't a magician. You want cheap conjuring tricks and theatrics – try Broadway.'

'I see sarcasm is included too,' she said, in a voice dryer than a Martini.

'Why, exactly, do you need to disappear?' I said, returning the gaze, drawing my eyes level with hers. They were blue pools of mystery.

'That's my business,' she said. 'Surely you'll respect my choices in what I reveal to you and what I don't?'

I shook my head slowly. 'Nope. I need to know the "why". While you're telling me, you might as well add the "who", the "what" and the "where". I'm not willing to break the law for you, unless you give me a damn good reason to.'

Kitty swung her legs down and lowered herself onto the chair opposite my desk. She took another breath, a deep one this time, like a mournful sigh. 'I'm from LA. I was – am – married to a guy called Fallon. Eddie Fallon.'

The name meant nothing to me.

I quickly glanced at the third finger of her left hand. There was no wedding band or engagement ring. But there was a tiny circle of white flesh where some jewellery had once been.

Her voice quivered, and she drew on her cigarette. Some flakes of ash fluttered onto her lap. She wiped them away with a flick of her wrist. 'He's a real bad one. It's what I liked about him, at first.' She looked at me. 'What is it about the wrong man?'

I ignored that comment. 'I'm a Brooklyn boy, born and bred, but I been out to your neck of the woods a few times,' I told her. 'Back when I was a cop, me an' some of the guys from the precinct used to head out to the west coast once a year. We got to like a watering hole called The Alley Cat, three blocks north of Mulholland Drive, heading up to the hills. Small, cheap, cosy. They had a coupla good jazz combos in there on Friday nights. You know it?'

'Sure I know it. Nice place. Eddie took me there once.'

'I guess it just don't rain enough in California for a guy like me,' I grinned. 'You can take the boy outta Brooklyn, but you can't take Brooklyn outta the boy.'

She was dismissive of my small talk. She wanted to speak about herself. Typical broad. Fair enough. I knew all about me already. I wanted to hear all about her, so I suppose we were both happy. I shut up and let her speak.

She continued: 'I was working as a cocktail waitress in Santa Barbara. Some other girls and I were hostesses at a party. Eddie's a businessman. He owns a casino, entertains a lot of clients –'

'Entertains?' I butted in.

'Not that kind of entertainment,' she hissed. Then her expression softened, in the way that only a dame's does when her mind drifts into the recent, happy past. 'Eddie and I got talking. We fell in love. We got married. That was three years ago.'

'But?' Feel free to call me a cynic.

'But,' she said, squashing her finished cigarette into the ashtray. 'He got jealous. Insanely jealous. If any men were unlucky enough to even breathe in my direction, Eddie would have them threatened, beaten up. Some of them disappeared. He may have had them killed. I didn't know for sure. But I had my suspicions.'

'I know the type. All too soon he started beating up on you too. Right?'

She nodded quietly. 'It wasn't so bad at first. I could hide the bruises with make-up.' Kitty shuddered, remembering. Then, her voice got louder, rising in an angry crescendo. 'But powder and paint can hide only so much. I nearly got away once, but he caught me. The rat beat me black and blue. He got more and more violent as time went on. I was a prisoner in my own home. I had to get away from him!' Her eyes misted with tears. She reached inside her handbag, rummaged around, pulled out a Kleenex and dabbed at her face with it.

I hate to see a dame cry. It ain't right. They sure do it a lot, but that ain't the point.

If there's one thing that really riles me up, it's paying the IRS every year. But if there's one thing that riles me up even more, it's a guy who beats up on dames. That's a special kind of lowlife. Those heels have to work hard to bring themselves up to gutter level. It makes me mad. Listening to Kitty, I could feel the blood boiling in my veins. And the veins stood out in my forehead, ready to pop like a kid's balloon being hit by a new pin. I clenched my left fist until it went white at the knuckles, fingernails grinding into my palm. I managed to control the rage that seethed inside me. 'And here you are,' I said, through gritted teeth. 'How did you escape?'

She sniffed, dabbing at her eyes once again. 'I worked the tables at the casino from time to time, so I skimmed some money from the totals every week. I did it carefully, biding my time, so it wouldn't be missed. Easy when you know how. Eddie was out of town one weekend last month, so I bribed his new driver to take me to the airport one day, saying I wanted to meet an old friend who was flying in from Miami. I left the poor guy waiting there. I hope Eddie wasn't too rough on him when he realised I'd flown the coop.'

'Don't sweat it,' I said, reassuringly. 'Boys like that can look after themselves.' I reached inside the drawer and took out the bottle of bourbon again. I unscrewed the cap, poured her a generous shot. 'Another drink?'

'No, thank you.' She pushed the glass away from her. 'I must be going soon.' Her eyes were slightly puffy where the tears had smudged her mascara, causing them to look black around the rims. She looked like a beautiful, melancholy giant panda, but without the fur. I liked it when dames wore make-up. They owed it to themselves to look good.

Kitty stared at me with those dark eyes. 'Eddie's after me. He's here, in New York. I've seen him, hanging around near my hotel. I don't know how he found me so fast.'

'It's pretty amazing the lengths a guy'll go to, the levels he'll sink to, whenever a pretty dame is involved,' I said. 'Especially when he's married to her.'

'Sounds like you're talking from personal experience.'

I ignored that comment too.

'It's only a matter of time before Eddie makes his move,' she said. 'He's crazy. He thinks if he can't have me, then nobody else can. I know for sure he'll kill me if he can't drag me back to LA.' Her soft voice became resolutely defiant. For a frail, she was pretty darned tough. 'And I'm *never* going back, Jack.'

'If I agree to help you, how do we work it?'

'Eddie has to witness my "death". The only way he'll believe it is if he sees it with his own eyes. I could arrange a meet with him, somewhere very public. Then we take it from there. I've got some ideas.'

So she had it figured. I mulled it all over in my head like a brainless TV game show contestant facing an easy question. I must have been crazy to take on domestic situations like this, but I really needed the folding green. Even if it was stolen from a psycho casino owner in LA. At least my reasons were noble, huh? One day, dames will be the death of me, I thought ruefully. 'Okay. I'll do it. You got yourself a deal.' I rubbed my chin thoughtfully, day-old stubble scraping under my fingers. 'It's late. I'm tired. Swing by here late tomorrow morning and we'll get ourselves a proper plan.'

She looked relieved, and grateful. She smiled. 'Thanks, Jack. You won't regret it. You'll be saving my life.'

'Saving it by pretending to take it,' I murmured, savouring the contradiction. But then, women are full of contradictions. It's what makes them women.

Kitty eased her skirt down where it had ridden up above her knee, showing another thrilling glimpse of creamy flesh under silk stockings. She got up to leave. 'I'm staying at the Broadway Plaza.' She handed me a gilt-edged business card. 'Here's the number.'

'Swell place. I hear it's expensive.'

'You needn't worry about your fee, Jack,' said Kitty, turning her head in my direction as she walked to the frost-glassed door. 'I got enough funds.'

'Kitty,' I mumbled. 'That's not what I meant –'

'No?'

Damn. She was right. It was exactly what I'd meant. I feebly tried to make up for it. Grabbing a pencil, I scribbled my home and office telephone numbers and home address onto a small scrap of

15

paper lying on the desk. I bounded over to the main reception door and handed it to her. 'Wait. Be careful. If Fallon turns up, call me. Anytime, day or night. By the way, what does he look like, anyhow?'

Without even thinking, she said, 'He's six five, 150 pounds, with brown hair, blue eyes, and a scar above his right eyebrow.' She glanced at the piece of paper before taking a second to stuff it into her bag. 'See you tomorrow, Jack.' Then she was gone.

I watched as her silhouette disappeared down the hallway towards the lift. I closed the door behind me, turning the key in the lock.

I retreated behind my desk, fished around for a fresh cigarette and lit up, breathing out a deep lungful of smoke. I pulled her abandoned glass towards me. It was still stained with a red smudge where her lipstick had been. I knocked back the bourbon. It tore at my throat. I leaned back in my chair and stared at the ceiling, contemplating what I'd gotten myself into. Kitty was really something.

Something beautiful? Very definitely.

Something dangerous? Very probably.

She'd sucked me into her game like one of these new fangled vacuum cleaners.

A sharp rap at the door snapped me outta my musings. I rubbed my eyes. Kitty musta forgot to tell me something important. Who else would be calling at this time of night?

I rose, and unlocked the door, smiling to myself, saying: 'Couldn't keep away. Huh, doll –'

I looked up and saw a coupla thugs grinning like Cheshire cats – ugly, vicious ones that wore dark suits and fedora hats.

A savage fist knocked the smile off my face.

Chapter Three

Uninvited guests

Dumb. I was getting sloppier than the post-lunchtime coffee at Pete's greasy spoon across from my apartment block.

Recently, I'd had too many late nights with only a bottle of whisky for company. Sure, booze is your best friend, at first. It makes a man forget the things he doesn't want to remember. Until he wakes up the next morning, and remembers what it was he was drinking to forget.

I don't even know what that meant.

My head hurt.

So did the rest of me.

A good private dick's always gotta have his mind on the job in hand. And my mind had been on Kitty O'Malley. More specifically, my mind had been on her legs. As of that evening – technically – she *was* the job, so I wouldn't beat myself up over it.

Besides, on that score, these two chuckleheads were doing just fine all on their own. The element of surprise, combined with my dopiness, had served them well. They'd laid into me before I'd got a chance to even put my dukes up. They'd sat me in my chair. One of them was big and stocky, and it seemed he'd lost his neck in the wash. He had piggy little eyes and jet black hair. The other guy was taller, with a tangle of reddish hair and dimpled cheeks. Both had fedoras jammed so tight on their heads it looked like someone had nailed them there.

Scott Montgomery

I hadn't actually passed out from their kicks and punches, but I pretended that I had. There was warm blood in my mouth. I could feel its metallic taste in my throat. My nose was crusted with dried blood, and my swollen right cheek felt like it had been inflated with a bicycle pump.

'He's out cold,' said No-neck.

'Careful,' said Dimples. 'Keep an eye on him.'

'Whoa. You in charge now, all of a sudden?'

'Eh? I was just saying –'

'I got this, all right? I was gonna keep an eye on him. Right before you said so.'

'Okay, okay. Fine. Keep yer shirt on.'

'Whassat supposed ta mean?'

'It don't mean nuthin'. It's just a figure of speech.'

'Then why'd ya say sumthin' if it don't mean nuthin'?'

Sheesh. It was gonna be a long night. I couldn't take much more of this. I let out a low, mock grunt.

'He's comin' round,' said No-neck.

'I can see that,' said Dimples, his voice irritable. 'What's with the running commentary anyways? You on the radio, or what?'

'This some kinda lovers' tiff?' I asked. 'If so, I can leave you boys alone.'

No-neck punched me right in the kisser. Bright spots of light danced in front of my eyes. I shook my head to clear the pain. So I asked for that one. People always said I had a big mouth. Now I had a brand new fat lip to go with it. I hawked and spat a mouthful of dark blood onto Dimples' right shoe. 'Oops. Clumsy of me.'

Dimples made a fist and punched me in the gut. I gasped like a burst paper bag, and lurched forward in the chair, winded. My chin hit the top of the desk. I rested there for a few seconds, struggling to get my breath back. If this was the alternative, then maybe the riveting conversation wasn't so bad after all. I slumped back in the seat, breathing heavily.

Dimples took the spotted cotton handkerchief from my left breast pocket and bent down to wipe his soiled shoe. He dropped the bloody handkerchief onto the desk, and squinted at me. 'Think you're a tough guy, huh?'

'Sure I do,' I said. 'Don't they teach you anything at Lowlife School?'

That remark earned me another punch in the midriff from No-neck. I was convinced I heard one of my ribs crack.

Dimples smiled, showing blackened teeth that resembled two storeys of condemned houses on Skid Row. 'I'm a quick learner. You keep talking, we keep hitting. A very simple lesson.'

18

The Long, Big Kiss Goodbye

No-neck balled his right fist into his left palm a couple of times. 'Lessons were never this much fun in grade school,' he said, looking pretty pleased with himself.

Aw, musta been his first witticism.

These boys weren't pros. That much was certain. They were trying real hard to act tough, but obviously watched too many movies. I was doing my best to provoke them, to see what they would do next. Real wise guys would've pulled guns on me by now, brandishing them like shiny new toys. Everybody wants to be a gangster these days. Hollywood has a lot to answer for.

I snorted, 'Who put you bozos up to this?'

Dimples walked round the back of my chair. He stopped behind me. Then he wrenched my head back, clutching my hair in one hand. He bent down, putting his face close to my left ear. 'Someone needs to teach you some manners,' he said in a hopefully menacing whisper. His foul-smelling breath seared the side of my face.

I ignored the pain in my scalp. 'And someone needs to teach you how to brush twice daily, pal.'

He scowled and let go of my head. He motioned for No-neck to come forward.

Now was my chance.

I forced my head backwards with all the strength I could muster. I caught Dimples right in the stomach. He pitched forward with a gasp. I elbowed him in the face, mashing his nose with a crunch of bone and cartilage. He let out a girly yelp and crumpled to the deck.

No-neck blundered towards me. I was outta the seat and ready to meet him. He swung for me, but I sidestepped and he caught thin air. I landed a sharp left jab into his considerable gut, then a right, both blows almost bouncing off the flab. He got me with a left hook to the jaw, but overbalanced. I brought my knee up into his groin. He howled in agony. Then I clasped my fists together and smashed them down on his head with all my might. He crashed downwards onto his stomach, rolled onto his back, and lay still. He was breathing. His chest was rising and falling in a regular beat.

I don't like to fight dirty. But let's be mature about this. They started it.

I picked up the bourbon bottle and held it aloft like a weapon. Dimples' puss was a mask of blood. His nose was spread over his face like a pancake with strawberry jam. He trembled. 'Please, man. No more.'

'You didn't answer my question,' I said. 'Who put you up to this?

Dimples tried in vain to stop his nose from bleeding, putting

19

Scott Montgomery

his fingers to his face. 'I dunno. Just some Joe. We never saw him before tonight. He gave us 50 bucks apiece to give you the treatment.'

'Well, I'd say you need some treatment yourself.' I still brandished the bottle, although I reckoned he'd had enough for one night. 'An' stop bleeding on my carpet, will ya?'

'Then you shouldn't have broke my goddamn nose, mister,' he whined, pitifully. 'You ain't gonna call the cops, are you?'

'Shuddup,' I growled. 'No cops. Now beat it, before I change my mind. Wake Sleeping Beauty there and get the hell out.'

'Thanks, mister,' said Dimples, meekly. He had lost all his unconvincing toughness from earlier. He kneeled in front of No-neck, slapping him in the face, gently at first, then harder. No-neck eventually moaned and slowly sat up. He got groggily to his feet. He kept his mouth shut. Probably the smartest thing he'd ever done in his life.

As they shambled towards the main door, Dimples looked like he was about to offer an apology.

'Out,' I snapped, before he had a chance to open his mouth.

Just before the defeated twosome left the room, I asked: 'The guy who paid you to work me over. What was he like?'

Dimples sniffed painfully. He stood deep in thought, trying to create a picture in his mind. 'Rich. Smart duds. Expensive shoes.'

'What did he *look* like?' I said, with more than a hint of menace in my voice.

'Okay, okay, okay.' Dimples shrunk backwards from my glare. 'A fella can't think straight when he's being intimidated.'

'Think harder,' I advised. 'And faster.'

No-neck was very quiet. He threw a look of pure hatred in my direction. I didn't have the time to wait on this genius coming up with any mental pictures.

Dimples, the brains of this outfit – which wasn't saying much – finally broke the silence. 'The guy was tall, well built. With dark hair; coulda been black, coulda been brown, I don't remember. I was too busy thinking about how I was gonna spend my 50 bucks. He had a scar above one of his eyes, that I do remember.'

I opened the main door. 'Take a hike. If I ever see you two round here again, you'll be on the deck with a chalk outline round about you.'

No-neck bunched his right fist. 'Why, you no good, lousy stinkin –'

Dimples stayed his hand. 'Forget it, man. This cat means it.'

'Yeah, well, me too.' The behemoth glowered at me.

I glowered right back. 'You're lucky I don't confiscate your new allowance. Go buy yourself a new neck.'

The big man hissed in my direction, exposing some blood-flecked front teeth.

They sullenly filed out. I slammed the door behind them, almost taking it off the hinges.

Eddie Fallon had paid them to do a number on me.

I was in a pretty foul mood. I didn't feel like driving, so I decided to leave my car overnight in the basement parking lot. It would be safe there. I figured a walk across town might help clear my throbbing head a little. Most people woulda thought I was nuts to go out on foot in New York at that time of night, but I didn't care. I retrieved my tan trench coat and black fedora from the hat stand. Locking the office door behind me, I took the stairs down to the ground floor. I lit a cigarette in the lobby and stepped out into the night.

A few stars hung in the ebony sky, sparkling like diamonds on black velvet. The night air was warm. A welcome, gentle breeze blew in my face. It cooled me down, causing my open trench coat to flutter behind me like a vampire's cloak.

Yellow street lamps bathed the sidewalks in a sickly, jaundiced glow. All around me, decrepit slum buildings towered upwards like they were fruitlessly trying to reach the heavens. Dozens of small squares of light illuminated grimy windows that held a myriad of life inside each tiny apartment. The neighbourhood was all ugly brickwork and battered, splintered front doors. I passed by a derelict building. It stood impassively, festering like a scab on an open wound. A few bums had taken up residence inside. They cried out some insane gibberish into the darkness.

The usual seedy lowlifes and scantily clad ladies of the night were out in force. The lowlifes tried to noise me up, but to no avail. I wasn't taking the bait, and I wasn't in the mood. Normally, I'd never walk away from a potential dust-up. One thing you shouldn't ever oughta do in New York City is back down. The way I saw it, though, this wasn't backing down. This was me doing them a favour. The hospitals were probably full enough already at this time of the evening. No-one seriously challenged me though. I musta been giving off some bad vibes.

The hookers stood on every street corner, trying and failing to look alluring; cackling like witches, hawking their sad wares. I got propositioned several times. I ignored them, and the nasty comments they hurled at my back. I strode on, things on my mind as I puffed at the cigarette, its red tip glowing in the dark.

If Fallon wanted to play games, then he'd picked the wrong opponent. Tonight's events had made me all the more determined to help Mrs Kitty O'Malley.

As I neared my block, I flicked the cigarette butt onto the

sidewalk, and got my keys ready. Behind me there was a screech, then the sound of a trashcan crashing to the ground. I whirled round, fists raised.

It was just a cat, some mangy thing out on the prowl for the evening. Its ginger and white fur was matted with dirt. Luminous green slits for eyes stared at me curiously. I knelt down and patted the scrawny animal on the head. It mewed quietly. 'Happy hunting, kitty,' I said, as it padded off into the night.

I let myself in, made my way soundlessly through the dark, deserted lobby and took the lift to the fourth floor. I opened my apartment door, stepped in and secured the chain across the lock behind me.

I was beat. Literally.

I hung my hat, coat and suit jacket on the floor and crashed out fully clothed on top of my empty bed.

Chapter Four

In the scheme of things

I woke late the next morning after a good night's sleep. I rubbed my eyes and felt around the top of the bedside cabinet for a cigarette. I found one and lit it hungrily.

Later, while I shaved, I noticed my left eye was a bloodshot purple and yellow bruise, my mouth was swollen and a couple of my front teeth were chipped.

I spent 20 minutes submerged in the bathtub, trying to rinse away some of the previous night's aches and pains. Luckily, my ribs seemed to be okay, if a little sensitive. Then I got dressed; light brown suit, beige shirt and black tie.

I called into Pete's for a breakfast consisting of fried eggs and bacon, grilled sausages, rye toast, orange juice and all the black coffee I could drink. The mouth-watering smells of frying food and freshly boiled coffee jolted me awake better than any alarm clock. I took my time with the breakfast, devouring every mouthful like a condemned man having his last meal.

Carla, the handsome, middle-aged waitress, was surprised when she saw the state of my face.

'You should see the other guys,' I said, guzzling a final cup of coffee. I paid the cheque, left a tip and went outside.

It was a cool day. I blinked, sunlight shining in my eyes as I made my way across town on foot. It was 11.30 when I finally made it to the office.

Scott Montgomery

Betty greeted me with her usual cheerful smile, then a look of concern when she noticed my face. 'Jack! What happened?' She was young, cute and eager to please. She was also efficient, hard working and made a hell of a cup of coffee – the perfect secretary. Her chestnut-coloured hair was a mass of tight curls that framed her freckled face. She had dark, brown eyes that stared from behind a pair of thick-rimmed spectacles, giving her the appearance of a baby owl. She wore a green cotton dress and matching shoes. 'Well?' Her voice was high-pitched and anxious, like she'd been breathing in helium all morning.

I hung up my trench coat and fedora. 'Don't worry, sugar. It ain't nothing. Just a slight disagreement with a coupla guys last night.'

'You do disagree with a lot of people.' She rose from behind her immaculately-tidy desk and stepped towards me. She started fussing, pawing at my swollen cheek. 'Oh, Jack. Lemme see. You need someone to take care of you.'

I gently waved her outstretched arm away, and said with mock indignation: 'Who are ya, my mother?'

Betty sat down again. 'You know, if only you'd let me, *I* could look after you, Jack.' Her voice was hopeful.

I leaned over the front of the desk and clasped her right hand in mine. 'You already do, sweet cheeks.'

I meant it.

She blushed hotly, her face turning an interesting shade of scarlet. Trying to hide her embarrassment, she scrabbled around the desk, finding the morning's mail, opened and date-stamped. 'H-here's your stuff,' she stammered, as I headed for my office. 'Jack, I nearly forgot–'

I turned round, curious. Betty never forgot anything.

'There's some broad waiting for you. She's been here for, like, half an hour.' Betty's voice was suddenly quiet. 'I suppose she's pretty, in a trashy kind of way.'

Good. Kitty was here.

I glanced at the telephone on Betty's desk. 'Hold all calls, Betty?'

Betty sighed. 'What calls?'

I closed the inner door behind me. Kitty was seated opposite my desk.

'Good morning,' I said.

This time, Kitty was wearing a low-cut cerulean blue dress that matched her eyes, and attracted mine like an industrial-sized magnet. A small, neat jacket – of the same colour – was draped over her shoulders. I noticed she wore tan stockings instead of black. Her legs looked even better than they had the day before. Her voice cut short my wandering thoughts.

'Is it still morning?' she replied, impatiently. 'I was wondering when you were going to make an appearance.'

I sat down. 'One of the few privileges of being my own boss.'

'Looks like you've had a run-in with Eddie.'

'In a manner of speaking.'

'I told you he was dangerous.'

I patted my pockets, looking for cigarettes, finding them in the last one. 'Did he attempt to contact you last night?'

She shook her head.

'I suppose he was too preoccupied with hiring guys to put me in hospital.'

Kitty seemed strangely unsurprised. I supposed she'd been through all this before. And she'd been the one on the receiving end. Out of the blue, she said: 'Your secretary doesn't like me.'

'Betty?' I asked. 'What makes you say that?'

Kitty smiled. 'Call it women's intuition. And the way she looked me up and down like I was the competition. Pure jealousy. You know she's in love with you, don't you, Jack?'

I stuck a cigarette between my lips, letting it hang there unlit as I spoke. 'So she and I had a coupla late night fumbles a little while back. Don't mean we're married.'

'You really know how to sweet-talk a girl.'

'No complaints so far.'

Kitty snorted in a derisory fashion.

I struck a match and lit my cigarette, exhaling a small, grey cloud of smoke towards the ceiling. I offered her a cigarette. She took one, and I lit it for her. She nodded her thanks.

'Do you have a gun, Jack?' she asked.

'Yeah, Smith & Wesson .38 revolver. A memento from my days on the force.'

'Can I see it?'

'It's at my apartment. I got a back-up piece here, but only for emergencies. I don't like guns. I try to avoid carrying one whenever possible. Guns are for cowards. They make little men feel big. I prefer to let my fists do the talking.'

She seemed impressed with my little speech. Then she said, 'Can you get a hold of some blanks?'

'Shouldn't be a problem. The local gun rack will have them in stock. It's a few blocks from here. Okay. What you got cookin', Kitty?'

Kitty blew some smoke out of the side of her mouth. She became animated, leaning forward with enthusiasm. 'Here's the plan. I find Eddie, and agree to meet with him. It has to be in a public place. I tell him that we don't want to cause a scene at the hotel, in case he and I get thrown out. You and I make sure it's somewhere a little less conspicuous, and a lot less classy.' She smirked. 'I'm sure you could recommend somewhere suitable.'

'Hilarious.'

'I was thinking maybe a diner; one with a history of being robbed, perhaps even somewhere near here. You burst in, armed and masked, and turn the place over.'

'Then what?' I asked, shifting in my chair awkwardly.

'I start to needle you. Rile you up real bad. Then you make an example of me.' She put the cigarette in her mouth, suspending it between her lips. She raised her right hand. She mimicked the action of a pistol being fired, using her right forefinger as the barrel, aiming it at me – like a little child at play. 'Bang.'

'Except, of course, the gun is filled with blanks.'

'Of course.'

'What about Eddie?' I said.

It was as if she took a weird kind of pleasure in describing her own fantasy demise. She completed the childish mime by blowing gently on her upturned forefinger, like someone clearing gun smoke from the weapon's barrel. 'That's the complicated part. You have to kidnap him. You take him prisoner after shooting me, and threaten everyone else. You tell them to get out of the building, if they want to live.' She drew on her cigarette, taking it out of her mouth with her right hand. 'Then you dump Eddie some place out of town, alive.'

'Easier said than done, if he's as crazy as you say.'

'I'm counting on your being able to ... improvise,' said Kitty. 'Eddie will then think that I've been the victim of a terrible, random incident, common in a city as big and bad as New York. A tragic case of being in the wrong place at the wrong time.'

'Yeah, and then he'll swear vengeance on the heel who murdered his wife,' I said. 'He'll be out for blood. My blood.'

'He won't ever find out that it's you,' she answered. 'Meanwhile, in the deserted diner, I miraculously come back to life, and high tail it to some place safe.'

'You'll need a death certificate.' I looked at her smiling face. 'Solid proof that you died, if Fallon should ever get suspicious.'

'I'm one step ahead of you,' she said curtly. 'I got a contact at the Coroner's office. He's promised he'd help me. For a price, of course.'

'Who?' I asked.

'A distant relative. He's a cousin of a cousin from my Mom's side of the family, or something like that,' said Kitty. 'They moved out here before the War.'

'This cousin of yours got a name?'

'Ritchie Vine,' Kitty said, impatience creeping into her voice. 'Feel free to check up on him. He's young, and greedy, and stupid, but what can I say? He's family.'

I frowned incredulously. 'And we all live happily ever after? You really think this dumb scheme will work?'

Kitty's cigarette smouldered between the forefinger and middle fingers of her right hand. A thin wisp of smoke rose upwards from the cigarette's burning tip. 'It's perfect,' she said, oblivious to my comments.

'Perfectly stoopid,' I hissed. 'It'll all go haywire. There's always a catch with scams like this. The rogue element that'll crop up on the day, something nobody coulda ever accounted for. It'll bring your clever little scheme crashing down, taking you and me with it.'

She swore under her breath and stabbed at the newly emptied ashtray with her cigarette butt, black ash staining white enamel. She got up to leave. 'Then I guess I'll take my business elsewhere.' Her voice was icy. Her nostrils flared in anger. 'See you around, Jack. Your cheque'll be in the post. Not that you've done anything to earn it.'

I sprang up from my seat and caught her roughly by the arm. 'Wait.'

'Let go of me!' she yelled.

I tightened my grip. 'I told you to wait.'

'You're hurting me!' she spat. Her lips curled in disgust. 'That what you're into, Jack? You like to hurt girls, is that it? You're no better than Eddie!'

I relaxed my grip a little. 'No, that's not it at all.' She was close to me. I could smell her. She struggled in my grasp like the frail thing she really was, although she wouldn't ever admit as much.

'Let me go, damn you!'

I stared at her angry, beautiful face. I didn't want to hurt her. I wanted to taste those ruby lips. I'd been longing to kiss her ever since I clapped eyes on her the night before.

She stopped struggling. Our eyes embraced.

At that moment, there was a quick, gentle knock on the door, and Betty walked in, her nose stuck in a file full of nothing. 'Sorry to interrupt, Jack, but it's important. About the Oysterman case –' She broke off when she looked up and saw Kitty and me looking very cosy together. 'I'll come back later. Maybe.'

'Betty, hang on.' I stepped away from Kitty. We looked like a couple of awkward teenagers who'd just been caught necking. I felt a tightening in my gut. But maybe that was something to do with the cooked breakfast I'd chowed down earlier. Bacon does strange things to a guy.

'It's lunchtime,' Betty snapped, without looking me in the eye. She stormed out of the room, slamming the door behind her. That door was taking a pounding these days.

Kitty was more relaxed. Obviously she had enjoyed my discomfort. 'You handled that well,' she sneered.

'Betty'll come round,' I said, to myself more than to Kitty. 'She always does.'

In a situation like that, a minor crisis on my hands, I did what any other self-respecting sleuth would have done. 'Fancy a drink?' I asked Kitty. 'I'm buying.'

Chapter Five

Never get involved

Barley's was my favourite Downtown drinking den. Not that I'd visited every one for a comparative study, of course, but I'd given it my best shot.

It was on the corner of Cedar Street, situated in a small basement that some people might have unkindly termed 'dingy'. Personally, I preferred 'atmospheric'. A circular stone staircase with black metal railings on the right hand side wound down from the sidewalk, leading towards a little corridor lit by a few, slowly disintegrating candles crowned with flames that fluttered in the wind outside. The corridor led into the bar itself, permanently half-lit by a discoloured, yellowing light bulb that hung from the ceiling like a hangman's noose.

'It ain't the Waldorf Astoria,' I motioned around with a mock flourish. 'But I like it.'

There were stools at the semi-circular bar, several conspiratorial booths, small, circular wooden tables, rickety chairs, and a dilapidated pool table. Grimy wallpaper and flaking brown paint were the décor of the day, or had been for at least the last ten years. The smell of sweat, warm beer and stale cigarettes hung in the air, mixed with the aromas of urine and disinfectant that emanated from the men's room.

A motley crew of young and old, although mostly old, men sat around drinking, enveloped in a fug of cigarette smoke. The place was popular with immigrants – especially the Scots and Irish, because it reminded them of little pubs back home.

'It's ... cosy,' Kitty lied, trying her best to be tactful.

The regulars stared at Kitty like she had just crawled outta the Black Lagoon.

'Quit gawping, you guys,' I said. 'Ain't ya ever seen a dame before?'

Okay, considering the way I'd been eyeballing Kitty since I met her, then maybe that remark was a tad hypocritical. I never said I was consistent.

'Naw. No' like hur,' drooled Iain Campbell, the young Scottish souse who, a year previously, had stowed away on a ship from Glasgow and woken up in Staten Island Ferry Terminal after drinking himself unconscious for several days. 'Whit a darlin'. Did she gie ye that shiner, Jack?' He motioned towards my black eye, slurring in that impenetrable Glaswegian accent, raising his beer glass as he spoke. 'If so – cheers, hen.'

'None of your business, Campbell,' I smiled. 'Client confidentiality.'

A little chorus of 'Wooooo,' whistled round the bar.

Some guffawing followed, and a schoolboy snigger from Campbell. 'She looks pretty confident tae me. Heh.'

Kitty grinned, taking it all her stride. She liked all this attention. 'A girl's lucky to find herself in Mr Sharp's capable hands.'

A small cheer went up, then a round of applause.

Big Al McKee, the barman, had been clearing some beer glasses from the tables. He was a jovial figure, overweight, with an ample gut ballooning over his trouser waistline, and with thin strands of greasy black hair stuck to his balding pate. He was clad in the usual grubby apron that had presumably once been white. An equally grubby white dishcloth was draped over his right shoulder like a bandolier. Al walked over to the bar, a couple of glasses clinking in each hand. He put the glasses down. Opening the latch set in the chipped mahogany counter, he stepped behind the bar, and set it down again. 'Hey, Jack. What'll it be?' he asked me, but winked in Kitty's direction. 'Don't worry 'bout the guys in here, Miss. They're a decent bunch, really. Harmless.'

'I'm not worried,' said Kitty. 'And beer is fine for me.'

'Make that two, Al,' I said.

His voice was like gravel. 'Comin' right up.' The big man set to work at the beer tap, swirling some amber-coloured ale into a newly-cleaned tumbler.

Kitty and I wandered towards a small, vacant table and sat down. I sat with my back to the wall. Kitty sat in front of me. A single candle, jammed in the top of an empty beer bottle, lit the table. Tendrils of hot wax had dribbled down the sides of the bottle, hardening into little pearly lumps on the smooth wooden finish of the table. A full, foul-smelling ashtray was the only other ornament. I leaned forward onto my elbows, causing the table to wobble to the left hand side.

Why do bars always have at least one wobbly table? Maybe there's a municipal law about it. Maybe I was the kinda guy who always picked the wrong table at the wrong time. Or maybe *every* table was wobbly. What with this being America, and all things being equal, maybe every table in every bar in every city all had a fundamental right to wobble. Or even worse, perhaps there was some kind of table conspiracy. Every wobbly table could potentially cause us to spill our drinks, ensuring that we buy more and more booze, turning us into a nation of brain dead, beer-swilling bozos who never question the reasons why there's always a wobbly table in the bar...

Ever find yourself thinking too much about stuff?

Now, what was I saying?

Oh, yeah. We were at the table.

Al was waddling over with a glass of foaming beer in each meaty hand.

I fumbled around in my inside coat pockets and my fingers brushed against the small box of a dozen blank cartridges that I'd bought at the gun rack on the way. I found my wallet in another pocket, plucked out a couple of dollar bills and held them at the ready for Al.

The barman dumped the glasses down onto the table, which lurched to the left like a ship hitting an iceberg. Beer spilled over the table, leaving a warm, wet circle underneath each of the glasses.

'Sorry,' mumbled Al. 'Why's there always a wobbly table?'

Don't worry. I won't start on that again.

Al slung the dishcloth from his shoulder and wiped the rickety table for us.

'Thanks, big guy.' I handed Al the money. 'Keep the change.'

He looked at the notes in his podgy hand, smiled, and stomped back to his counter.

Kitty raised her glass.

I raised mine and we clinked them together. 'Cheers,' we both said at the same moment. I eyed the amber liquid, the minuscule bubbles rising, popping at the foamy surface. Kitty watched as I took a long drink, enjoying the cool taste as the beer slid down my throat. I put the half-empty glass back on the table. 'I needed that.' I could feel some foam on my upper lip.

Kitty smiled her mischievous smile. She leaned towards me. Once again, her pretty face, her pale skin and the swell of her chest transfixed me. 'You got a little beer moustache.' She brought her slender right hand up to my face. Using her forefinger, she wiped at my mouth, slowly, gently. It was the first time that her skin had touched mine. Her hand caressed my mouth and upper lip. A barely audible scratching noise issued from my recently-shaved face as her fingers made contact. I closed my eyes, letting her touch engulf my senses. I took her hand in mine and held it as gently as I could. Her hand trembled. I opened my eyes, gazing into hers.

She snatched her hand away. 'Jack. I – I can't. Not now. Oh, I don't know anything anymore. It's this business with Eddie. I –' She broke off, lowering her gaze, eyes darting around self-consciously. She reached for her own beer and took a long, hard drink. 'I'm sorry.'

'I'm sorry too,' I said, although I was lying through my teeth. I still wanted her, even though she was clearly in a mess. One minute she was giving me all the signs, the next she was brushing me off quicker than a clump of dandruff on a black suit. I sighed.

We sat in silence, drinking our beer. I drained my glass. 'Time to go.'

Nine hours later, we were still there.

Kitty had made the fatal mistake of offering to buy me a beer.

Kitty and I, we'd drunk ourselves back sober. We talked and smoked cigarettes. Then we talked some more. I told her about my time on the police force. She told me about LA, and about Fallon.

'One more for the road, Al,' I said, almost knocking over the wobbly table as I stood up, opening my near-empty wallet.

Al was sweeping the floor, ready to close up for the night. 'I think the road's had enough, Jack,' he said, leaning against his broom in one hand, rubbing his tired eyes with the other. 'And so have you. Don't you and the little lady have somewhere to go?'

'One more little, itsy-bitsy, tiny drink, Al,' said Kitty. 'What's the harm in it?'

Al positioned the broom against the counter. 'Honestly, folks, I would if I could, but it's closing time.' He threw a sympathetic grin in our direction. 'Trust me. I do this for a living.'

'Come, ma'am. Let us leave this place,' I said, pretending to be insulted.

Kitty got up too. I draped my trench coat around her shoulders. 'Why, thank you kindly, sir,' she said, smiling.

She could handle her liquor. Impressive. For a dame.

I shook Big Al's hand, his massive paw almost breaking my fingers. 'Take care, Al. G'night.'

'Goodnight, Jack.'

Al turned to Kitty. He took hold of her right hand, bent down and kissed it softly. 'A pleasure to meet you, Miss.'

'It was lovely to meet you too, Al.' She beamed up at the big man. She stood on her tiptoes and struggled to peck him on the cheek. 'Goodnight.'

He grinned and waved goodbye as we headed for the corridor that led outside.

If Wall Street was New York's brain, then Manhattan was definitely its heart. Life pulsated along the sidewalks like blood pumping through arteries.

Even though the streets were lit up like a giant, over-decorated Christmas tree, blinking on automatically every night with garish efficiency, it was a place that drew people like a magnet, hopeful that something, anything could happen here.

Ambient traffic noise and the sounds of voices carried on the September air. The night was warm enough not to be winter, but cool enough not to be summer. Kitty was feeling cold. She huddled in my trench coat, pulling at the lapels, drawing them closer together over the front of her chest. 'I don't feel like walking.'

'Me neither,' I replied.

A steady torrent of traffic, including some telltale yellow blurs, whizzed past as we stood on the sidewalk. I stuck out my arm and managed to hail a cab first time. The grubby yellow car nearly ran over my foot as it skidded to a halt in its owner's eagerness to pick up the fare. We clambered in the back and I told the Hispanic driver to take us to the Broadway Plaza.

Normally, it was quite a long cab journey to the Theatre District, but not the way this maniac drove. Like most New York cabbies, he obviously never understood what a car's gears were actually for, crunching through them like he was in charge of a wrecking ball. He never even slowed down when he hung a sharp left onto Broadway. The engine groaned, protesting like a stroppy kid dragged to the shops by his mom. A coupla snooty-looking theatregoers had to duck outta the way of our car.

I changed my mind about this cabbie. I liked his style.

Unsurprisingly, he liked Kitty, taking every opportunity to ogle her legs in the rear-view mirror, and smiling a gleaming-toothed grin when she caught him at it. She just looked bemused. 'Keep your eyes on the road, fella,' she purred.

We skidded to a halt right outside the Broadway Plaza with

the screech of tyres in our ears and the smell of burning rubber in our nostrils. I paid the driver and gave him a decent tip. 'Thanks, man,' he said slowly, nodding his appreciation. He lasciviously ogled Kitty one last time before driving off at high speed, swerving to avoid more irate pedestrians. A small circle of black smoke belched from the cab's exhaust pipe.

Kitty rolled her eyes at the retreating vehicle.

Broadway stretched out in front of us. It was an effervescent thoroughfare of hopeful dreams and empty promises. The hollow beauty of the seemingly endless billboards, theatre buildings, bright lights and sounds of the shows still took even my breath away. You couldn't help but be seduced by the glamour, even though you knew there was always sadness, loneliness behind the glitz.

The Plaza was an impressive building. Its beautiful, art-deco façade towered over us, with intricate carvings set in stone on the balcony directly above the main entrance. Above the carvings, a massive Stars and Stripes fluttered in the wind on its golden flagpole, jutting at right angles from the wall.

Kitty and I ascended some polished marble steps, sandwiched between a couple of large plant pots holding exotic bushes that stood impassively to attention like sentries. A gaunt, middle-aged doorman was positioned at the top of the staircase, arms clasped behind his back like they were handcuffed there. He wore a burgundy coat with gold epaulettes, a matching cap and white gloves. I suppose years of being on the force had taught me to get as much detail as possible, in as few words as possible. It was a hard habit to break. The doorman doffed his cap as we approached. 'Evening, ma'am.'

Kitty smiled but didn't answer.

The doorman frowned in my direction, barely acknowledging my existence.

'What ho, Jeeves,' I muttered as we walked past him, through the glass revolving door and into the main lobby. A thick burgundy carpet was beneath our feet. The lobby was like a cathedral. The opulent décor consisted of more creamy marble; finely stitched rugs; plush leather chairs; elegant circular tables, with vases full of fresh flowers on top; and brown silk drapes adorning the windows.

I wasn't accustomed to this type of hotel. I was as out of place as a snowdrop in Harlem.

We ambled over to the marble-embossed reception area. It was like all hotel reception areas: a raised desk with an immaculately tidy office space, with everything in its correct little place, right down to the paper clips in the bureau. There was the illusion of busyness, but in reality, a whole load of not very much happening. The atmosphere was probably supposed to be welcoming, but this had backfired worse than a Beretta with a cork jammed in the barrel.

A sour-faced female receptionist, who wore too much make-up and had jet-black hair tied back into a severe bun, was glued to the seat behind the desk.

Kitty and I both rested our elbows on the raised plinth, and Kitty asked for the key to room 604.

The receptionist looked me up and down. 'We have a strict policy here. No visitors in guest rooms after midnight, *sir.*' The last word was accompanied by a venomous smile.

'Well, doll,' I growled, not in the mood, 'I got a strict policy of reporting uppity staff to the management if they yank my chain.'

She ignored that. She swiped the correct key from its little hook on the board against the wall and handed it over.

'Have a nice evening,' I said, doffing my fedora as we made for the lift. 'Try not to smile too much.'

The receptionist's icy face looked like it might crack at any moment.

Kitty pressed the button for the lift, and we quietly waited as it made its way down from the thirteenth floor, taking what seemed like an eternity.

'I can manage on my own from here, Jack.'

'Sure you can,' I said. 'But I'd rather see you up to your room safely, if you don't mind.'

'Of course I don't mind.' That coy grin was at the sides of her mouth again.

The lift lumbered down towards us. The doors slid open with a bright 'ping' noise. We got in and headed for the sixth floor. 'You need to speak to Fallon early tomorrow morning, and arrange to meet him for lunch at Earl's Diner,' I said. 'It's on the corner of West 53rd Street and Seventh. It's been turned over a few times this year. Just the kind of place you're looking for.'

'West 53rd and Seventh,' she repeated. 'Okay.'

We arrived on the sixth floor with a gentle jolt and another 'ping.' Kitty led the way to her apartment, down a corridor with white, glossy walls. We took a left turn, then right. She held a forefinger to her lips as we walked. 'We'd better be quiet.'

'I walk the way I walk, Kitty. I only skulk around hotels when I have to.'

Kitty unlocked the door to room 604, twisting the key and withdrawing it slowly. 'Do you want to come in, Jack?'

'Just for a minute.'

'What?' Kitty laughed quietly. 'You think someone's hiding in my bathroom?'

'Maybe,' I grunted.

She shuddered slightly when she realised I was being serious.

We stepped inside. I went first, with Kitty behind me. I pressed the nearest light switch. It was certainly a pretty room: magnolia walls with white borders; plush beige carpet; four-poster bed; varnished writing desk and chair; a divan in the corner, with a coffee table in front of it. A lamp stood on top of the bedside cabinet on the left hand side. The bathroom was on the right side of the room. I stuck my head in and flicked the electric light on. It was empty.

A pair of ornate wood and glass doors, with tasteful, patterned curtains, led to a veranda outside. A narrow shaft of moonlight shone through the gap in the curtains like a torch beam.

'Nice,' I said.

'Can I fix you a drink?' Kitty asked, taking my coat from her shoulders and throwing it down onto the bed.

'No, thank you,' I said. 'I'd better go. We've got a long day ahead of us tomorrow.'

'Maybe I've had enough to drink too,' she said. 'It's been a fun day.' She fanned at her face with a dainty hand. 'The maid must've forgotten to leave a window open. I need some air.'

She was right. The room was way too warm. I loosened my tie and top shirt button a little.

Kitty walked over to the doors and opened them. She stepped out onto the veranda. A cool breeze blew into the room, causing the curtains to sway slowly, as if moved by unseen hands. 'It's a beautiful evening,' she called out to me. 'Come see, Jack.'

I followed her out to the veranda. The bottom edges of Kitty's blue dress fluttered in the wind. She tilted her head back, exposing her bare neck and throat, breathing in the cool night air, letting the breeze caress her skin and gently blow at her blonde hair. 'Spectacular view,' I agreed.

I wasn't talking about the skyline, although it was pretty impressive too.

New York sprawled in front of us. I drank in the view like a tourist at the top of the Empire State. Crystalline skyscrapers and rectangular tower blocks spread out in every direction, as far as the eye could see. The dark blanket of sky enveloped the legions of buildings, like waves crashing relentlessly against rocks. A perfect crescent moon hung in the heavens, surrounded by glittering stars.

I could even make out the dull outline of the Brooklyn Bridge, and the thousands of tiny pinpricks of light that marked out Coney Island, my old stomping ground. Home sweet home.

I stood behind Kitty. She was still gazing towards the stars. 'You're beautiful,' I whispered.

She turned towards me. 'What did you just say?'

Even I wasn't sure what I'd just said. 'The view, it's beautiful.'

She was very close to me. Again I felt the deepest thirst for her welling up inside, threatening to overwhelm me. My heart was thumping, blood rushed in my veins. I wanted her so bad it hurt.

And she knew it. That was the worst part.

I looked into her cold, blue eyes. And saw only my own desire reflected there.

'Do you want to kiss me, Jack?' she said, softly.

'You know I do,' I said. 'More than anything in the world.'

'Then why don't you?' She pursed her scarlet lips, closing her eyes, expecting my mouth to invade hers within an instant.

I sighed. 'The golden rule of detective work is "never get involved".'

Her eyes blinked open in surprise. 'When I met you yesterday, you said you didn't follow the rules.'

'Well, maybe it's about time I started.' I pushed the brim of my fedora backwards, away from my forehead. I suddenly grew interested in my shoes. I studied them intently, rather than look her straight in the eye. 'You're my client, Kitty,' I explained. 'As a professional private detective, I'm responsible for you, and your safety. I can't let my personal feelings get in the way of a case. I'm sorry.'

'I'm sorry too,' she said, her voice low.

This tense moment was a strange mirror image of our awkward words in the bar earlier. We'd both apologised for our feelings then too.

There was a low rumble from above, and a few raindrops pattered down on us, gently at first, then building steadily.

'There's a storm coming,' I said.

Kitty didn't answer.

Soon, rain battered the rooftops in an unrelenting, unforgiving downpour. It fell in thick sheets of water, drenching everything in its path, streaming like a sudden pall of misery from the dark clouds that now hung over the city. Thunder rumbled menacingly in the obsidian sky, illuminated by staccato bursts of lightning.

'It's amazing how quickly people can change,' said Kitty, as we headed back inside. 'Just like the weather.'

'I should go, Kitty. Goodnight.' I headed towards the door.

I could feel her eyes searing into my back, like flying saucer laser beams from a cheap science-fiction movie. I closed the door behind me, thundered down the stairs instead of taking the lift, and strode through the lobby, out into the rain.

Five minutes later I was in the back seat of another yellow taxicab, listening to the rhythm of the rain pounding on its roof, heading home alone to my apartment.

Chapter Six

Involved

A loud thump at the door woke me.

I sprung out of my dream. I won't tell you what I was dreaming about. My head throbbed from too much booze and my throat burned from too many cigarettes.

Three more thumps shook the door, in quick succession, like pistol shots.

As my sleep-gummed eyes struggled to adjust to the dark, I could just make out that the clock near the bedside read 3.00 am or thereabouts.

I reached under the bed and grabbed my .38 out of its holster, secured under the bed frame with duct tape. The rubber grip was cold as I held it in the palm of my hand. I quickly checked the load – six bullets, one in each chamber, right where they oughta be. I spun the cylinder and snapped it shut. The persistent banging at the door grew in volume and intensity. I brought the gun up, pausing only to flick off the safety catch as I crept towards the door.

I took position at the side of the doorframe, clasping the pistol in both hands, the four-inch barrel pointed towards the ceiling. 'Who is it, and what the hell time do ya call this?' I growled, sounding like the Big Bad Wolf – only armed, dangerous and very annoyed.

Silence.

I thumbed back the gun hammer, chambering a round with a quiet click.

'Jack?' asked a familiar voice. 'It's me. Kitty.'

I wasn't taking any chances. 'You alone?'

'Of course.' Her voice was edgy, impatient. 'You going to let me in?'

I pulled at the door chain with one hand, the gun in the other. 'Hold on,' I said as I wrenched the door open.

Kitty stood in the doorway. I looked around the corridor, quickly making sure she was on her own. She had a small bag slung over one shoulder and was soaked to the skin, trembling. She flinched at the sight of the gun in my hand. I had the gun pointed down towards the floor now. I brought it up, thumbed the hammer back into place and reapplied the safety catch. I bundled her inside the apartment and shut the door.

'What's wrong, Kitty?' I said. 'You all right?'

Her face was pale. Her wide eyes stared at me. Her hair was saturated with rain, smeared against the side of her head. Raindrops dripped to the floor from her wet clothes. She was scared. For the first time since I met her, she looked vulnerable. 'Eddie paid me a visit right after you left. He threatened to bust the door down if I didn't let him in.'

'What did he say?'

A few strands of wet hair had fallen into her eyes. She brushed them away, blinking. Her voice was anxious. 'Like I thought, he wants me to go back with him to LA. He said it's my final chance. I can go back with him alive and well, or in a pine box. It's my decision.' She shivered uncontrollably.

I led her towards the sofa. She flopped down into it, exhausted. She looked around the apartment, seeing the detritus of grimy dinner plates, stained coffee cups, dirty laundry and old newspapers. 'Look at this place. It's been ransacked. Who would do such a thing?'

'Who knows? Guy in my line of business makes a lot enemies.' I didn't have the heart to tell her that the place hadn't actually been turned over. I was just a slob. I nodded at her shoulder bag. 'What's that?'

'Some clothes. Just in case you thought I shouldn't go back to the hotel.'

'Good thinking.' I nodded. 'When I finally meet that heel Fallon, there's gonna be trouble.' A red mist of anger was descending upon me. 'He'll never threaten you again. I'll make sure of that.'

'I told him I'd go back with him, but he had to collect me at Earl's Diner tomorrow. Just like you said, Jack.'

'You did great, Kitty.'

'I got so spooked when Eddie turned up. I thought he might come back again. I don't how he managed to get past the hotel staff.' She paused for a breath. 'He must've been spying on us, and knew when you'd left.'

'Yeah, I think you're right.'

We both suddenly realised I was dressed in only my boxer shorts, with a loaded weapon in one hand.

Kitty's gaze followed me as I went to the bedroom. I slipped the gun back into its holster under the bed. Then she averted her eyes as I hastily threw on a white vest and hopped on one leg as I struggled into a pair of pants.

I nodded at the open kitchen door. 'I'll make some cocoa to heat you up. You'll catch your death –'

At that, she started to cry. Tears welled in her tired eyes, glistening on her already wet cheeks. 'Oh, Jack!'

In view of what was going to happen the next day, my choice of words had been as subtle as a brick through a window. 'Kitty, I'm sorry,' I said dumbly. 'I didn't mean to say that.'

'Jack. I don't want to be alone tonight.' She got up on her feet, but stared towards the floor. She looked up at me. 'Can you ... hold me? Just for a little while.'

I rushed over and gently pulled her close to me. 'Don't worry,' I said. 'This'll all work out fine.' I could feel her body tremble beneath my touch. Her heart pounded in her chest.

'Jack, I'm sorry,' she stammered. 'I didn't know what to do.'

'Relax,' I said. 'It's okay. You're here now.'

She grasped my hand in hers and brought it up to her face. 'I feel so safe here with you.'

I embraced her once more. 'I'm not normally like this with my clients.'

She smiled at that.

We gazed at each other; two people who needed, wanted, yearned to be together.

Then it finally happened. Our lips locked together in a kiss so electrifying it could've caused a citywide blackout. The ever-present scent of her perfume was still in my nostrils, as was the musky heat of her body. It was intoxicating. Our hands explored each other hungrily. I could feel the smooth flesh beneath her wet dress. She gasped with pleasure, yielding to my every touch, my every caress. We kissed again, and again; her hot, sweet breath pounded in my mouth. She clasped me closer, crushing me against her. I put my lips to her exposed neck, nuzzling the soft skin, letting my mouth travel down to her collarbone. She quivered with delight. Then she jammed her mouth against mine. More frantic kisses followed. Her tongue writhed inside my mouth like an electric eel out of water. I was powerless to resist her. We

Scott Montgomery

couldn't stop even if we'd wanted to.

Then she pushed me away from her. A smile played upon her scarlet lips.

'Don't, Kitty,' I said, shaking my head in disbelief. My voice sounded pathetic, like a petulant child's. 'Don't brush me off again. I can't stand it anymore!'

She put a finger to her lips. 'Hush.'

I watched, fascinated, as she grasped her flimsy, damp dress and ripped it open. It made a wet tearing sound, falling downwards, buttons scattering across the floor. I gazed wide-eyed at the contours of her body: the thrust of her breasts against the black silk brassiere as they rose and fell in time with her breathing; the voluptuous curve of her hips; the stocking-clad, creamy delights of her thighs; and the fleshy treasure between.

'So,' cooed Kitty. 'What about "the golden rule of detective work," Jack?'

'To hell with the rules.'

We kissed once more, hot, sensual and lingering. I felt light-headed, giddy with desire. I took her in my arms, sweeping her off her feet in one easy movement. She giggled like a debutante as I carried her towards the bedroom.

A rectangular outline of early morning sunlight pierced the drawn curtains, slowly bringing me to my senses.

Had I dreamt the wonderful events of the previous night?

I stretched out my left arm, hoping to find Kitty lying by my side. I patted only cold, crumpled bed sheets. I rubbed the sleep out of my eyes for the second time in a few hours. If it had been a dream, then I didn't want to be awake.

Click.

The blood ran cold in my veins. I knew that sound. It was unmistakable – a gun being cocked. Not only that, I knew right away that it was my gun. I dunno how to explain it. As much as I dislike firearms, using them only as a last resort, there's something special about the police issue revolver, and the way an officer lovingly takes care of it. He gets to know the weapon intimately, protecting it as if it were a dame. I'd stripped, cleaned and oiled that medium frame, carbon steel gun so often, I knew the sound of every click of the cylinder, hammer and trigger.

Very, very slowly, I raised my hands. Never make sudden movements when someone has a gun pointed at you. Without breathing, I looked round.

Kitty was sitting in the chair opposite the bed. Her hair was tousled. Her face was pasty, without make-up. Her eyes were bloodshot. She was wearing my white cotton shirt from the previous night.

And she had my .38 in her right hand. Thankfully, she wasn't pointing it directly at me, but the weapon was loaded, primed and ready to kill.

It was as if Kitty was in a daze. She had a vague, confused expression on her face. She fiddled with the gun like a kid with a birthday present.

'Kitty,' I said, 'put the gun down.'

'Just wondering,' she whispered, 'what it would be like to shoot that rat Eddie.' She brought the revolver up in my direction. 'Bang, bang. You're dead.'

I could feel my heart beating faster, thudding against my ribcage. I offered her my hand. 'Kitty, give me the gun. Please. Someone could get hurt.'

'I'm already hurt!' she screamed. 'All because of him.' Her eyes became cloudy with tears. 'It's all *his* fault.' Her face was a collage of sadness and hatred.

'I know,' I said, soothingly. 'I know. Just give me the gun, and we can talk about it over breakfast. Just you and me. What do you say?'

She pondered this for a moment.

My heart was beating so loud, I wondered if she could hear it too. 'Kitty,' I repeated, nodding at the gun. 'Give it to me. Please?'

She looked at the gun in her right hand, eyes widening in horror. 'What am I doing, Jack?' She turned the weapon over in her palm. Her hand started to shake. She offered the gun to me, hands unsteady.

'Good girl.' I took the pistol from her erratic grip, flicked open the cylinder and emptied out the bullets. Six live shells cascaded downwards, clinking towards the wooden floorboards like a little fountain of brass. I tossed the gun onto the bed beside me and breathed a sigh of relief.

Kitty buried her face in her hands. 'Jack, I'm sorry,' she mumbled into her palms. Then she started to cry once more; quietly, then much louder; great big sobs of sadness.

I reached for her, and held her close. She wrapped her arms around me, rocking back and forth like a child. 'It's okay,' I said. 'Everything's going to be okay. I'll make sure of it.'

'You promise?'

'I promise.'

Chapter Seven

Death of a dame

Late morning sunlight glinted from the tops of buildings as I eased the car out of the dark parking lot and into the traffic. The street was heaving with cars of all shapes and sizes. The whiz of traffic, confrontational voices and the impatient toots of car horns all combined to form a burgeoning symphony of ambient noise. Pedestrians crowded the sidewalks, striding ahead, ignoring each other like extras from a movie crowd scene.

The aroma of gas fumes and the smell of my beloved Buick Roadmaster's leather upholstery filled my senses. My breath had misted the interior windshield, so I wiped at it with a small, damp chamois I kept in the glove compartment. The engine was always reluctant in fall weather, so I had to give it some choke before I finally got moving. I built my speed up slowly, until eventually I was cruising along steadily in third gear. I fumbled to light a cigarette with one hand, keeping the other on the steering wheel. I rolled the window down a little, letting in some fresh air that blew through my hair as I moved along.

Folks think a private dick should drive a flash car. I beg to differ. In this business, a top-notch ride was the first thing guaranteed to bring unwanted attention from both the law and the lawless. This nondescript, beige 1948 sedan was a popular model, and it had served me well on tail jobs, surreptitiously blending into the streets like a chameleon on a branch. And the chunky vehicle's eight cylinder, 16-valve engine was sturdy and reliable.

I made sure I didn't drive too fast. I couldn't afford traffic cops on my back.

I hadn't bothered going up to the office. Betty could keep the place ticking over on her own for now. I'd apologise to her once the case was closed. It would all be over soon.

It was good to be back behind the wheel. It was good to feel in control.

Kitty's presence had distracted me; put me off my game. Yeah, dames usually had that effect on me. But not like this. I wasn't sure I liked the way that Kitty made me feel. I recalled what had happened that morning.

Neither she nor I had spoken much over breakfast. We sat quietly in the living room. I'd tried to tidy the place a little while she had been in the bathroom.

I'd made a pot of rich, tar-black java and scraped some butter on a few slices of white toast.

I couldn't take it any longer. I broke the awkward silence, saying: 'We've got a lot to do. Before you meet with Fallon.'

Kitty looked up from her chipped, ceramic coffee mug, swirling the steaming contents around. 'Yes,' she said solemnly.

'Are you nervous?'

'I guess so.' Her voice had been distant. Like she was talking through a bad telephone connection.

'Kitty,' I said, gazing at her. 'I know you've taken a lot recently. But we can only get through today if we're prepared and focused. This is a dangerous game we're playing.'

'I know what I have to do, Jack,' said Kitty. She smiled, but it was a hollow smile. 'After today, I'll be free of Eddie. That's all that matters to me.'

'Right.'

Part of me wanted to ask, 'But what about *us*?' I shook the thought from my head.

'I'll give you and Eddie about 15 minutes together before I come in. It'll be difficult, I know, but try to relax and act normal. We don't want him getting suspicious.'

Kitty watched as I strapped a leather shoulder holster over the top of my shirt, under my left armpit. I went to the bedroom and brought the revolver from under the bed. Then I retrieved my trench coat from the stand in the hall and fished out the box of blanks. I drew one of the bullets out like a cigarette from its pack. It had a dull zinc tip and a standard brass casing, which reflected a small dot of light against the wall as I turned it around in my fingers.

'These beauties are just what we need.'

The bullet seemed to interest Kitty. She started to speak, but her voice was a whisper. 'When you ... shoot,' she hesitated. 'Will it hurt?'

'No. You won't feel a thing.' My voice was a low, reassuring burr. 'The actual sound of the gun going off will probably frighten you much more. Makes one hell of a racket, especially in an enclosed space. I won't stand too close when I fire. I don't wanna deafen you.' I flicked the gun open and loaded it up with shells. 'Most people prefer automatics these days,' I noted. 'But they jam too often for my liking, and they leave too much evidence; casings everywhere. Good when you're the cop, but not when you're the perp.'

Kitty nodded, understanding. She held up her mug. 'This coffee's great,' she said. 'Could I have another one?' She seemed reassured, happier even.

'Absolutely,' I smiled. 'Comin' right up.' I stood up, making sure the pistol's safety catch was in place before placing it on my seat. I picked up the coffee mugs and headed for the kitchen.

I'd come through the bustling, beautiful, crazy hive of activity that was Times Square, and was now deep into the seamy side of Manhattan – a maze of shady backstreets full of gambling dens, dusky whorehouses and grimy gin joints. It was all too easy to believe that this tragic burlesque was within walking distance of the shallow opulence of Broadway and 42nd Street.

Now I swung the car into a small, abandoned alleyway off West 53rd Street, just opposite Earl's Diner. Tyres groaned beneath the chassis as I manoeuvred the car round in an awkward U-turn, so that it was facing the street. I switched the ignition off. I sat smoking in silence for a moment. I got out of the car, leaving the driver's side door unlocked. I took a final draw on my cigarette before letting it drop to the sidewalk, extinguishing it under my heel. I could feel the tremor of the subway beneath my feet, rumbling into the distance. A cloud of vapour hissed through a nearby manhole cover.

I stepped round to the back end of the car and popped the trunk, bringing out a pair of black leather gloves, a small, brown leather satchel and the mask. It was a kid's plastic Halloween mask – Lon Chaney as the Wolfman. I stuffed it into my right-hand coat pocket, put the gloves on, and slung the satchel over my left shoulder. I slammed the trunk down with a thump that shuddered through the vehicle.

I crossed over the road to Earl's. Its glass façade looked out onto the sidewalk. Approximately one third of the front window was obscured by a large, printed menu and chalked billboard. A coupla patrons sat at a small table, looking across at each other, chatting and slurping at large, frothy milkshakes through straws. I loitered outside, like I was consulting the menu.

Then I took a few steps back, towards the barbershop next door, trying to look like I was waiting on someone. On the inside, a fat man was seated at the window, getting shaved. Half his face was still covered in shaving cream. The other half was clean and smooth. Luckily he was too busy yapping away to the smartly dressed barber standing behind him to notice me.

I ducked into the narrow lane between the barber's and the diner. It was littered with garbage and old newspapers and stank to high heaven. Obviously the local winos had been using it as a bathroom of late. Satisfied that the lane was empty, I got out the mask and pulled it over my head, attaching it into place with the little string of black elastic. My face felt hot beneath the plastic, my breathing heavy and loud. The eye slits were restricting my peripheral vision slightly, but that couldn't be helped.

All going well, Kitty had met up with Fallon 15 minutes earlier.

I glanced at my wristwatch. It was 1.45 pm. Showtime.

I reached to my left side and felt the .38's rubber grip. I took a deep breath, drew the gun and flicked off the safety.

Astonished staff and customers looked up in disbelief as I barged into the diner and held the gun aloft. I must have looked a fairly ridiculous figure with that stupid mask on, so I fired a single warning shot towards the ceiling to get their undivided attention, letting them know that I was deadly serious. The loud report of the shot echoed around the room. 'Listen up!' I yelled. My voice sounded like someone else's, a menacing growl muffled behind the mask. 'This is a robbery. Everybody down on the floor and you won't be harmed!'

The panic started right away. Women and children were screaming. The cacophony of noise mixed with the hiss of steam, the sizzle of steaks and the aroma of fried onions, causing an all-out frontal attack on the senses.

Holding the gun in my right hand and the satchel in the left, I scanned the room, looking for Kitty, and saw her at a table near the counter, sitting opposite a swarthy man. No prizes for guessing who he was.

An old geezer, standing behind the counter in a crumpled, white waiter's uniform, slowly moved towards the telephone against the wall. I pointed the gun at him and shook my head like a disapproving parent. 'Naughty, naughty, Pop,' I said. 'Hands up. Now.' I felt bad scaring the old guy like that, but I had to keep up the act. I motioned towards the cash register with the pistol. 'Open it and empty it. You know the drill.'

'Sure I do, you rat,' said the disgusted old timer; his wrinkled face wrinkling even more.

'You got guts, Pop,' I said. 'But they'll be decorating the wall unless you open the damn register.' I threw the satchel down on the counter. 'Fill'r up.'

The rheumy-eyed old relic hit a button on the register and it sprang open with a loud *kerching*.

I stood on the spot and turned 360 degrees, brandishing the .38, scanning round the room, making sure no-one was trying to sneak up behind me. Everyone kept their heads low, staring at the floor. Now the stench of sweat filled the already ripe air. 'That's it, folks,' I shouted. 'You're doing great. Keep your heads down and we'll all get through this in one piece.'

The old man was slowly filling the satchel with wads of used notes, grubby tens and twenties by the look of them.

'C'mon, Pop,' I growled. 'A little faster. There a safe in here?'

'Y-yeah. In there.' He paused from filling the bag, jerking his thumb at a heavy storeroom door behind him.

'Open it,' I ordered. 'After you empty that register.'

Pop hurriedly swept the rest of the cash into the satchel, which now bulged with money. He fumbled nervously under the counter.

'I'm watching you, Pop. No funny business!'

That made him even more nervous. 'I-I'm just getting the key,' he stammered. 'Don't shoot.'

So far, so good. I looked at the table adjacent to the counter. Kitty sat there. She looked up as I walked over.

'Whatcha starin' at, lady?' I tried to disguise my voice, making it as gruff as possible.

'Nothing,' she said, quickly. She grimaced at me. 'Nice doggie.'

Fallon was seated opposite her. He had dark, brown hair swept back to the temples; murky blue eyes; a small, vertical white scar above the right eyebrow; an elegant, Roman nose, with slightly flared nostrils; a nasty mouth set in a sneer; and a blue shadow of stubble across his chin. He was handsome in a stark, brutal way. He was wearing an immaculate, grey pinstripe suit, with a matching waistcoat and golden watch chain suspended from the right-hand pocket. He also wore a starch-collared white shirt with a light blue tie. Now he was playing the part of the concerned husband. He reached across the table and held Kitty's hand. 'Don't provoke him, honey.'

The thought of that sleaze – the man who had beaten Kitty, forced her to flee from him – touching her, reassuring her, made me mad. I tried to shrug it off. 'Listen to your man friend, *honey.*' Behind the mask, beads of perspiration stung my eyes. Damn, it was hot.

Fallon rose slowly from his chair, arms out in front of him in a placatory fashion. He was tall. Well over six foot. 'Hey, fella,' he said, and his voice had a rough, sandpaper edge. 'Can't we talk about this?'

'Nope.' I shoved the gun barrel close to his face. 'Now sit back down before I blow your smarmy mouth off, hero.'

He sat back down.

I stole a quick glance over to the counter. 'Hey, Pop, how's that safe comin' along? I'm growin' as old as you out here.'

'I'm trying to open it, honest, mister,' said a faint voice from inside the storeroom.

Now it was time for Kitty's act. She stared through the eye slits in my mask. 'Why don't you leave him alone, you coward?'

'Kitty –' started Fallon.

'Zip it, you,' I warned him. I turned to Kitty. 'What did you just say?'

'You heard. Where do you get off, threatening old men?' she hissed, then swept her eyes around the diner. 'And terrorising innocent people?'

She was doing well. I had to keep reminding myself that I was the bad guy here. It was like being back in the school playground: cops and robbers.

There was an uneasy, jagged silence as amazed customers took in the sight of this brave woman squaring up to the masked villain.

'Just for that, you can give me your purse.' I pointed the gun right at her, calmly chambering a round with a heavy click of the hammer.

'Go to hell. You'll get nothing from me.' Her face was defiant, full of hate.

'That's not nice,' I said, shaking my head with a mock tut-tut sound. 'Look's like I'm gonna hafta make an example of you.'

Fallon whirled his head round, frantically pleading with his wife. He grabbed at her arm. 'Kitty. What are you doing? Stop this. He'll kill you!'

Kitty pushed his hand away, ignoring him completely. Her gaze was level with mine. 'Do your worst, you piece of filth!' she spat.

A cold sheen of sweat enveloped my back. I could feel damp patches under my arms. My finger hesitated on the trigger, hand trembling. I couldn't shoot a woman. Dammit, I couldn't even pretend to.

'Do it!' she screamed.

I pulled the trigger. Once. Twice. Three times. The blasts were deafening. The reek of gunpowder and cordite filled the already stinking, humid air of the diner. A plume of grey smoke rose from the pistol barrel. I lowered the weapon, suddenly aware of yet more screaming from terrified patrons.

I glanced at Kitty. She was slumped back in her seat. Her eyes were glassy and lifeless, staring towards the ceiling.

Struggling to breathe behind the mask, I gasped in horror at the sight in front of me.

Three bullet holes had punctured her blue coat. Each one leaked a ghastly red, spilling down the front of her chest.

Kitty was dead.

And I had murdered her.

Chapter Eight

Cut to the chase

I was in shock. I stood rooted to the spot, dimly aware of people near me.

Fallon was beside her. He leaned over and put a hand to her chest. It came away stained with crimson. He stared at his red-smeared fingers, and looked up at me with pure, insane hatred in his eyes. 'Whoever you are, you are a dead man!' He shook with rage and lunged towards me. 'You hear me? Dead!'

I was jolted out of my showroom dummy routine. I reacted instinctively, bringing the gun up and firing another shot at the ceiling. As I'd hoped, it caused a scene of pandemonium all around. People started screaming again and tried to escape, bustling for the main doorway.

Fallon tried to follow me but got lost in the throng like a swimmer fighting against the tide. His words rang in my ears as I retreated: 'I will hunt you down and kill you, if it's the last thing I do, you slime-ball!'

I stuffed the gun into my coat pocket, vaulted over the counter and headed for the kitchens, where there would hopefully be a back door.

'Hold it right there!' said a frail voice behind me.

I whirled round, seeing Pop the decrepit waiter brandishing a ridiculous double-barrelled blunderbuss that was nearly as ancient as him. He must've had it stowed under the counter. His liver-spotted hands held the weapon unsteadily.

Marvellous. An octogenarian hero. Maybe he'd been a cowboy in his younger days. I didn't have time for this. But I didn't want to harm anyone else. 'Whoa. Put it down, Pop. Before you hurt someone.'

'I saw you kill that girl.' His voice, and his hands, trembled. 'You goddamn sicko. You're gonna pay.'

He had two shots in that museum piece.

That meant I had to move fast. I turned and ran for my life.

He pulled the trigger: twice in quick succession.

I fled towards the heavy kitchen door, expecting a barrel load of buckshot to rip through my back at any moment. The shotgun reports were like cannons going off in my mind. I dived, rolled forward and came up running once more. The top half of the door had blown apart, shredded into scorched splinters of wood and shards of glass, one of which lodged itself in the back of my leg, just under the knee. A sharp stab of pain surged through me. I could feel warm, sticky blood soaking my trouser leg. But I was still alive. Miraculously, the satchel with the loot was still hanging round my shoulder. Tiny glass fragments crunched underfoot as I bolted through the kitchen as fast as I could. Behind me, I could hear the old man snapping the rifle breech open and the tinkle of ejected shell casings on the floor.

I barged past a young chef who had been lying low, out of the way of the commotion. He recoiled in fear at the sight of me. 'Out the way!' I yelled, making for another wooden door that led outside.

I emerged into bright sunlight that momentarily blinded me. I wrenched the mask from my sweat-saturated face. I was at the back end of the diner, in another grubby alleyway. My car was across the street. All I had to do was get to it. Simple.

Then my heart sank as I heard the low growl of a disengaging car engine and the sound of a handbrake clunking into place. I turned to see a black-and-white NYPD radio motor patrol car pulling up and juddering to a halt beside me. Two-way radios had been introduced a few years back, and as a result, squad car response times to crime scenes were much faster. But even the fastest squad car in the local motor pool couldn't have been as quick as this. That meant it was an RMP out on routine patrol.

Typical.

Two cops were inside the car. The one in the passenger seat rolled down the window. He had fair hair and a tubby face. His jowls wobbled as he spoke. 'Hey, you. What's going on in there?'

'Wow! Am I glad to see you guys, officer! It was awful. A masked man burst into the diner.' I put my hands to my face, tried to look distressed and spoke in a high-pitched, nasal whine. I wasn't gonna win any awards for my acting, but these two didn't look the most shining examples of New York's Finest. I tried my best to sound even more hysterical. 'He-he-he threatened everyone with a gun, and he shot some poor woman! I managed to escape out the back! I think he went that way!' I pointed in the opposite direction to my car: towards Central Park.

'What did this guy look like?' Tubby's partner asked, leaning over from the driving seat. He was much thinner and had dark hair and a neat moustache.

'Well, he was wearing a mask, officer.' I said that with just a hint of sarcasm. 'I didn't get a good look at him. But I think he wore a grey flannel suit, and he had dark hair.' I held up the bulging leather satchel for them to see. 'He dropped this! I found it on the ground in the alleyway.'

Real decent of me, huh? Even though I'd just added "murderer" to my resumé, at least I wasn't a common thief. I'd always planned to give the loot back anyway. That was someone else's money.

'Give it here,' ordered Tubby.

I handed the bag over as meekly as I could. 'Y-Yessir.'

Tubby unzipped the satchel, saw the wads of cash inside. He turned to Moustache. 'Call this in. We'd better go take a look.'

Moustache nodded, reaching for the two-way radio receiver beneath the dash. 'Despatch, this is Car 4/5. We have reports of an armed robbery at Earl's Diner ...'

Tubby got out of the car slowly and waddled towards the diner, the cash bag in one of his piggy little hands.

Moustache followed him, slotting his nightstick into his belt. 'Back-up's on its way.'

'What about me, officer?' I whined.

'Stay right there for now.' Moustache turned his head towards me as they walked away. His voice was dismissive, figuring that a wimp like me wouldn't be any trouble. 'We'll be back in a minute. You'll need to make a statement.'

The cops strolled towards the front of the diner like they were on a Sunday school outing. If I'd still been on the force, I'd have had those two clowns up on a charge quicker than the time it took for Tubby to swallow a doughnut. What were they thinking of? Leaving a witness or possible suspect hanging around like a kid outside a candy store! It worked in my favour though.

A little group of agitated people were congregated at the diner entrance, chattering among themselves. I couldn't see Fallon. I'd worry about him later.

I waited until Tubby and Moustache were level with the crowd before I ran across the street, dodging past several cars on either side.

I got in my car and fumbled at the ignition. The engine chugged for a couple of seconds then died. I slammed my fist against the steering wheel in anger. Concentrate. I tried the ignition again. The engine caught second time around. I slid the clutch to the floor and moved the gear stick into first. I stomped my right foot on the accelerator and the vehicle tore forward. I swung the steering wheel in a tight arc, hanging left and out into the street. Tyres squealed, and the car was filled with the acrid smell of burning rubber. I straightened the wheel and headed Downtown.

My mind was reeling; thoughts collided in my head like pool balls on green baize. I couldn't think straight. My head was pounding. My hands trembled against the steering wheel like those of a souse opening a fresh bottle of whisky. Talking of which, I could've done with a drink.

Focus, Jack.

Just what the hell happened back there with the gun? I had checked the weapon myself that morning. It was definitely filled with blanks, dammit! I wracked my brain for an answer, finding none immediately. I'd worry about it later.

I had been driving on automatic, purely by instinct. I was so wrapped up in my thoughts that I hadn't noticed the speedometer. I was doing 60 miles per hour. I put my foot to the brake, felt the engine slow down. But it was too late.

The inevitable happened. A police car spotted me and moved onto my tail. The cop gave a quick blast of his siren, the signal for me to pull over.

Terrific. Just what I needed.

I'd gotten lucky with the two Keystone Cops back at the diner. There was no way that I'd manage to bluff yet more of the boys in blue. There were traffic signals at a crossroads on the road ahead. There was no-one in front of me. My light was red.

I floored the accelerator and surged forward with an ear-shredding screech of tyres, zooming across the road.

The cops took a couple of vital seconds to realise what had happened, and the squad car lurched forward unsteadily.

I wrenched the steering wheel round, swerving to avoid an oncoming station wagon. The other driver swerved too, or we might've crashed right into each other. Despite this, I still clipped the side of his vehicle. Metal ground against metal, sparks flying. The station wagon went straight on in the opposite direction. My passenger-side wing mirror was gone. It could've been worse.

I glanced into my rear-view mirror. A second squad car fell

into place behind me, siren blaring. And then another followed suit.

I made a quick, and doubtless very dangerous, decision. I bumped the car up onto the sidewalk. The vehicle lurched wildly. I was probably killing the suspension completely, pounding the engine into submission. I tore up the street, in the direction of the Upper East Side. The cops wouldn't dare to follow me onto the sidewalk, so that would buy me some time. I tried my best to avoid it, but I smashed right through a newsstand on a corner, causing an eruption of newspapers into the sky. Thankfully, the vendor dived out of the way in time. A coupla guys at a hotdog stand had to jump out of my way too. This had been a bad idea. I had to get off the sidewalk before I killed someone else. I blasted on the horn, signalling for people to get out the way.

Then I took a right onto East 79th Street. Next, another right turn where I pulled the steering wheel so hard I thought it was gonna break off in my hands. A hubcap flew from one of my wheels, bouncing down the street as I bumped the speeding car back down onto the main road. Terrified pedestrians jumped for cover as I zigzagged through the busy streets for about a mile. Buildings blurred past; the car shook violently as I navigated the labyrinth of backstreets and alleys. I'd been lucky so far. Amazingly, no-one was injured as my car hurtled down the narrow roads. I'd managed to shake the cops on my tail. They'd be back soon though.

I had to double back upon myself, so that I'd be heading Downtown, and it would probably confuse any cops on the lookout for me. I took a sharp left in third gear, and then another, so that I was facing south once more. I was now on Lexington Avenue. Finally, a lucky break, I thought to myself, breathing a sigh of relief. There was a decent-sized parking lot at the back of the Art Museum where I could ditch the car for now. The sound of screeching brakes echoed through the tall granite buildings as I stopped the battered vehicle just round the corner from the delivery bay out back.

I could probably bluff the cops into thinking that the car had been stolen, whenever they got round to tracing the vehicle back to me. Lame, I know, but almost believable. I got out of the car and slammed the door shut. It wasn't too badly damaged, apart from the wing mirror, a few new dents in the bodywork and the missing front hubcap on the driver's side. With a bit of luck, the police wouldn't find it here for a little while. I needed time to consider what to do next. I had to get my head together, freshen up and have a look at my injury. I'd have to get out of these clothes and dump them some place. I now had a long walk ahead of me, which would take even longer with my gammy leg.

I eventually managed to get back to my building without attracting any more attention to myself. I didn't want Winston, the nosey-parker building superintendent, to see me, so I snuck up the fire exit staircase. When I finally got back to my apartment, I locked the door behind me. I shrugged off my heavy coat, ran into the kitchen and poured myself a stiff bourbon, some of it sloshing against the worktop. I devoured the drink in one swift gulp, then poured another and downed that too, wiping my mouth with the back of my hand. The liquor scorched my throat and warmed my belly. I shuddered, thinking of the diner; me firing the gun, the bullets slamming into Kitty's chest ... It was like a recurring nightmare, replaying the afternoon's awful events over and over in my mind's eye. Then I felt my stomach turn, my guts somersaulting.

I lurched towards the bathroom and barely managed to kneel down in front of the toilet bowl before I violently retched a torrent of dark vomit down the U-bend. Sweat dripped from my forehead and into my eyebrows. My watery eyes felt like they were gonna pop outta my head. Then I wheezed, choking for a breath. I was sick some more; dry bile heaving upwards from the pit of my stomach. I sank back, exhausted, lolling on the cold, white tiles of the bathroom floor.

I realised I'd almost forgotten about the gun, so I limped towards the living room and picked up the abandoned coat. I had to examine the spent shells, find out what had happened. I was convinced there was one round left. I was sure I'd fired only five shots. I reached inside my coat pocket for the .38, and then swore loudly, not believing my bad luck. My pocket was empty. The gun was gone.

Chapter Nine

Dark reflections

I hunched over the sink in the bathroom and let the cold-water tap run for a few minutes. I cupped some water in my hands and brought it upwards, splashing it to my face. I let the water run down my neck, dripping towards the tangle of chest hair that sprouted from my stinking undershirt. I tried to rinse the acidic taste of vomit from my mouth, but it stubbornly remained, like a stain at the bottom of a coffee cup.

My fevered mind wandered back to that morning: Kitty and me sitting in the living room; me offering to make coffee ... It dawned on me then. I'd stupidly left the gun in the room with Kitty. She could have secretly switched the blanks for live rounds. But why on earth would she have done that?

Suicide by proxy? Nah. She'd wanted to fake her death, not die for real, although that was what had happened. The only thing I could come up with was this: maybe she had been hoping to provoke me into shooting Fallon instead. That would've got him off her back once and for all. And then she'd have had the cover story of it happening in an armed robbery. That almost made a twisted kind of sense. Then a dark, paranoid thought hit me like a right hook to the gut. Kitty could then have turned me over to the law: and her husband's evil murderer would have been out of her hair too.

No way. Remember I said that I thought about things too much?

I stood up straight and studied myself in the mirror, barely recognising the sallow face that stared back at me from the grubby glass. My green eyes were red-rimmed and bloodshot, with dark bags forming underneath; my black hair was greasy; my cheeks were puffy; my chin was flecked with a blue bristle of stubble; and my lips were grey and bloodless. I looked like I could've haunted the place. And I wondered what it might have been like to be a ghost. Wandering around an empty world, unable to touch, unable to feel.

I banished those dumb, self-pitying musings to the back of my mind when it dawned on me once again that I wasn't looking at the face of a wraith. I was looking at the face of a murderer. Sure, I'd seen people die every other day when I was a policeman. I'd killed three perps myself in the line of duty. I wasn't proud of the fact. It was an unavoidable, horrific reality, one that had always stayed with me throughout the years; but I hadn't been anywhere near as bad as some of my ghoulish fellow law enforcers, who had kept a running score of their own personal body counts.

Captain Frank Garfield was in charge of Homicide Division at the 47th Precinct, so this case would become his. He was a good man. He had a tough hide and a foul mouth, was hard but fair. He was also trustworthy and highly efficient; an all-too-rare combination these days. Back then, I'd seen cops on the payroll of the mob, or running their own protection rackets, and Frank never stood for any of it on his turf. He'd hunt me down all right. Maybe I should save him the shoe leather. I considered turning myself over to the cops there and then.

My gun must've been lost when the old geezer fired on me at the diner. Garfield's boys would find it at the crime scene. They would trace it and find it licensed in my name. Pretty soon they would tie it to the beige Buick that had given the local patrol cars the run-around straight after. And though the chief suspect had been masked and there were no fingerprints at the scene – 'cos the felon had worn gloves – even the dimmest rookie on the duty roster that day couldn't fail to deduce that it all led back to me; a nosy, smart mouth private dick who needed to be taken down a peg or two into the bargain.

How could I have been so dumb?

It was ironic that I'd been the one who'd lectured Kitty about the rogue element – the one thing that would go wrong on a score. Turned out it had been me all along. It was my fault that Kitty had died. And now it looked like I had a one-way ticket to the gas chamber. Told you dames would be the death of me.

But there was also Eddie Fallon.

Newsflash: a vengeful, mobster widower is not a good thing to have on your tail. He hadn't seen my face, but he knew about my connection to Kitty. He was a loose cannon, and it seemed to me he had balls. Maybe he might hurt some other people on his one-man blood hunt. I couldn't let that happen.

I took a deep breath and smelled stale sweat and dry vomit. I splashed more water on my face and quickly tried to freshen myself up a little. I stripped off my clothes, dug out a clean shirt and suit and threw them on in a hurry. Then, I stuffed the dirty clothes into a laundry bag and tied it tight. I'd dispose of them later. I went into the bedroom and held up the mattress with one hand, feeling around underneath for the 100 bucks I had stashed there for emergencies.

I thought about my limited options. I had to get out of there pronto. Any second, the flatfoots would be kicking the door in.

My office was also out of bounds for now. The next place the cops would look, for sure.

Then it finally dawned on me that there was someone who could help me out of this sorry mess I'd gotten myself into.

Chapter Ten

Sanctuary

Betty took one look at me and slammed the door in my face. Couldn't say that I really blamed her for still being in a foul mood with me.

She lived on the twelfth floor of one of the new blocks in the Lower East Side. It was a vibrant, promising neighbourhood. New building codes had cleaned up a lot of the slum housing and, thankfully, the area was no longer seen as just another dumping ground for immigrant families.

It hadn't taken me too long to get there, making sure that I avoided the main streets, just in case the cops were on my trail.

The obnoxious young caretaker slouched behind the desk in the lobby hadn't liked the look of me, so I'd backhanded him a ten-spot and suddenly everything had been hunky-dory and I'd been his new best pal. Although, he'd droned at me, technically, he really shouldn't have allowed a visitor to go up to Miss Stewart's apartment without checking with her first.

It was a nice enough building; clean and tidy, with plain, wooden décor and upholstery. It was fairly quiet. I could hear the usual sounds of radios and conversations and arguments coming from inside the three other apartments on the landing.

I spoke to the brass doorknocker on Betty's red apartment door. 'Betty. Open up, please. I need to speak to you. I want to apologise for the way I've been acting recently. I'm sorry.'

'Yeah?' Her angry voice was perfectly audible from behind the heavy door. 'Go be sorry some place else, Jack.'

'C'mon, Betty.' I rapped my knuckles against the door as gently as I could. 'Can I come in? I really need to talk with you.'

'Well, I don't wanna talk to you.'

I sighed.

The door to the apartment opposite creaked open, and a pair of beady brown eyes peaked out from the dark. The eyes belonged to an old lady's face: with cracked lips, wrinkled cheeks, a bent hooknose, a helmet of silver hair tied back in a tight bun, and a hairy mole on the folds of saggy skin that made up her neck. She cowered behind the door, giving the impression that all that remained of her was a disembodied head.

'Ma'am.' I tipped my fedora in her direction.

'Who the hell are you?' Her voice was rougher than mine.

'Just a visitor, Ma'am.'

'You'll need to speak up,' she scowled, showing teeth that jutted from her mouth like twisted enamel tombstones. 'I don't hear so good.'

'You don't look so good either,' I hissed quietly.

'You got a bad attitude, sonny.'

So you do hear all right, I mused. 'I'm just visiting Miss Stewart, Ma'am.' I said a little louder. 'No cause for alarm.'

'You a cop?'

'Not exactly.'

'Eh? What sort of answer is that?' She scowled once again. 'Either you are or you ain't.'

What was it with this old broad? She have trouble parking her broomstick today, or what? 'No, Ma'am,' I replied, polite, but insincere. 'I'm not a cop.'

'Well, you act like one.'

I shrugged.

She raised a wizened hand and pointed at Betty's red door. 'You leave that nice young girl alone. She doesn't need any more aggravation in her life. I've heard her talk about that loser of a private investigator she works for. If you ask me, she should tell that bum to take a hike.'

Yeah, well I didn't ask you, lady. But the oldster had a point. I was bad news. Always was. Always would be.

The old lady was still peeking at me through the narrow gap in her apartment door. She shrunk further back into the darkness of her stygian apartment, eyeing me with contempt.

'Bye, Ma'am,' I said, tipping my hat once more. I turned round, and began walking down the corridor, back towards the moving metallic cage that passed for a lift.

Then, from behind me, there came the sound of the sliding of a heavy bolt.

'Jack. Wait.' Betty's voice was low, quiet.

I came back along the corridor.

Betty was wearing a cream-coloured blouse, a long black skirt and black shoes. She looked like she'd just come home from the office. She regarded me sourly. 'You got five minutes.'

'Thanks, Toots –' I started. I looked round, seeing the old trout across the landing still staring at me.

Betty smiled at her. 'Oh, hello, Mrs Baines. How are you today?'

'Old,' she scowled. 'Same as I was yesterday. But thanks for asking, anyways.'

Betty gave another kind, but slightly strained smile.

Mrs Baines said: 'You all right, honey?'

'Of course.' Betty held her door open, nodding for me to go inside. 'I'm just fine.'

'Okay. G'bye then.' Mrs Baines eyeballed me with what I took to be suspicion, but was probably just plain, straightforward hatred. She retreated slowly into her own apartment. The door creaked ominously, like Nosferatu closing his coffin lid for an afternoon nap.

Betty's place was just like her: light and breezy and feminine. She led me through the narrow hallway, which smelled of fresh flowers and had dark blue carpets, and into the living room. The living room had freshly-painted magnolia walls, with a few landscape paintings and pictures dotted around; soft jade carpet; white davenport in the centre and matching chair on the left, with plush green cushions on top; tall lampshade on the right; a ham radio; gramophone, with records neatly stacked in a small display case beside it; wooden bookcase with three rows of books, mostly well-thumbed romance paperbacks by the look of the garishly-coloured, creased spines; and a little table with a vase of daffodils, the sweet aroma of which caused my nostril hairs to quiver.

Betty slumped down angrily onto the davenport, the cushions hissing with air beneath her round rear end in a comical way that she probably hadn't intended. 'So, where's your latest piece of white trash, Jack?

'Dead. And I killed her.'

Betty's face turned ashen grey in a heartbeat. 'What?' Her voice had raised an octave like it always did when she was distressed. 'Whaddya mean?'

I almost collapsed into the chair opposite, threw down my fedora, and confessed to everything that had happened since I last saw her the day before, although I glossed over the bit when Kitty and I danced the horizontal fandango at my apartment. I owed it to

Betty to be straight with her, but not that straight.

Afterwards, Betty looked shocked. She bit her lip, and then spoke quietly. 'So, did you enjoy it?' She didn't look at me. Instead she stared at the carpet.

'Enjoy what?'

'You know what! Making love to that hussy.'

She'd rumbled me right away. 'Betty, I don't know what you're –'

'Shut up, you ape!' Tears misted Betty's hazel eyes. Her voice was bitter. She struggled to speak, but made sure she got the words out. 'You always were a rotten liar, Jack. Men, you're all the same. You make me sick!'

'I didn't mean to –' My voice sounded pathetic, even to me.

'Oh, you meant it all right!'

'Okay, maybe us men are all the same,' I said, defensively. 'But you saw what she was like. How could any man manage to resist a woman like that?'

'You manage to resist a woman like me.'

'That ain't true. And it ain't fair, either.'

'What did you expect me to say, Jack?' hissed Betty. 'Well done?'

I put my head in my hands, rubbing my eyes wearily. 'You're right, Betty. I'm sorry. I shouldn't have come to you. I should sort out my own mess.' I got up to leave.

Betty got up too. She wiped a tear from her cheek. 'I didn't like her, but I wouldn't ever wish that on anyone.'

'I know,' I said. 'You're one in a million, Betty. There's nothing I'd like more in the whole world right now than to stay here with you, but I'm on the run. A murderer.'

'You never meant to kill her.' Betty took my hand in hers, looking suddenly, surprisingly calm again. 'She just hooked you in and used you. And like any typical, gullible man, you fell for it and went along with her dumb plan.'

Betty was totally right on that one. She was a smart girl. It must have been painful for her to swallow her pride and say those words. She understood me, and the stoopid things that I did. At least someone did. I grasped her hand tight. 'Thanks, Betty. If I manage to get out of this in one piece, I promise I'm gonna make it up to you.'

'Why don't you call the cops? Turn yourself in.'

'Maybe,' I said. 'But not yet. Won't take long for the law to trace me to you anyway.' I looked at Betty's questioning brown eyes. She wasn't wearing her spectacles. 'Don't worry, there ain't nothing gonna happen to you. I'll be outta your hair soon, Toots. Sorry to impose on you like this.'

'You're welcome to stay as long as you need. I'll make us some coffee.'

I nodded gratefully.

Betty walked towards the kitchen, her shoeless feet padding quietly on the carpet. 'What ya gonna do, Jack?'

Good question. I reckoned it was time to check up on Eddie Fallon and find out just exactly what kind of psychopath I was dealing with. 'Betty, would you mind if I made a long distance telephone call?'

Chapter Eleven

Where there's a will...

The female operator's clipped tones said, 'Putting you through now, caller.' There was a loud click.

'Yeah?'

I smiled at the monosyllabic drawl, picturing the portly figure about 2,500 miles away on the other side of the telephone exchange. He would be slouched in his chair, in an air-conditioned office, wearing a Hawaiian shirt with patterns louder than a fog horn, khaki shorts that showed off his fat, hairy legs, and leather sandals that didn't aggravate his bunions. I could picture his tanned, leathery complexion, crowned with close-cropped grey hair. He would have an unlit, half-smoked stogie clamped between his lips, chewing on it like a cow eating the cud in a field.

'Will?'

'Depends.' The voice was momentarily suspicious. 'Whoosis?'

'It's Jack.'

'Heh-heh!' Will Preston's gnarly voice erupted into a deep, throaty chuckle. 'How you doin' Jackie-boy?'

'I'm good,' I lied. 'How's Martha?'

'She's still married to me, so as well as can be expected, all things considered.'

'Miracles never cease.'

'You still in the PI racket?'

'It pays the bills,' I said. 'Sometimes.'

There was a pause on either side of the line.

'So,' said Will. 'We never were much good at small talk, Jack. What can I do for you?'

'Just a little intelligence, if you don't mind,' I said. 'Some information for a case I'm working on. No leg work involved.'

'No problem. Lemme get a pencil.'

I heard him rummage around his desk for something to write on. 'Fire away.'

'Ever hear of a guy called Eddie Fallon, or his wife, Kitty, probably going under her maiden name – O'Malley?'

I could hear the scribble of a pencil on paper. 'Nope. Should I have?'

'He's a hothead casino owner out in your neck of the woods.'

'Lotsa casinos in LA, Jack.'

'I know, buddy. Just see what you can uncover.'

'What's going on?' Will's interest was piqued. 'Anything exciting?'

I was poised to tell him, but decided against going into too much detail over the phone, just in case. 'Exciting? Hell, yeah. Let me know what you come up with: as soon as you can, pal. I owe you one.'

'Again.' Will's voice boomed into my left ear. 'Sure thing, partner.'

'Here's the number you can reach me on.' I squinted at the telephone dial, rhymed off Betty's number and hung up the receiver.

Betty came back in, carrying two steaming mugs of her legendary coffee. I took a sip from mine, and felt better right away.

'Who were you talking to?' she asked.

'Will Preston, my ex-partner,' I explained with a grin. 'The man was a great cop, but five years ago he stopped a bullet in a liquor store robbery, protecting a bystander. He survived, but decided to quit the force while he still had the chance. He had just married his childhood sweetheart, so they started a new life out west. He works as a bondsman in Hollywood now.'

'You must miss him,' said Betty.

'Yeah, but getting out was the best thing he ever did. You get guys like that. Ones who make the right decisions.'

The wait for Will to call back was an agonising one.

Betty and I talked for a while, but, selfishly, I wasn't really in the mood for chit-chat.

The phone rang after about 20 minutes, but it was only Betty's mother calling for the daily update on whether or not her beloved daughter had found herself a nice, decent young man yet. I grinned as Betty rolled her eyes to the ceiling while she listened to the story of the latest so-called eligible bachelor that her mother was intent on setting her up with. I could hear Mom yakking away; the voice was like one of those endless, high-pitched squeaks from the cartoons.

After a while, I switched on the radio, turning the dial in all directions, looking for Dave's Medium Wave – my favourite jazz station – but to no avail. I did, however, stumble across a local news report:

'… After an attempted robbery and alleged shooting incident at a diner in Manhattan earlier today, police are on the lookout for anyone with information leading to the arrest of a masked suspect, who was rumoured to have been driving a beige, 1948 Buick. The vehicle was found this afternoon …'

Wonderful. I switched it off.

'That ain't good,' said Betty's voice at my shoulder. She'd just come off the phone.

'You mind if I smoke in here, hon?' I asked.

'Go ahead.'

I rummaged in my jacket pocket for cigarettes and matches. As I found one and lit it, my spirits sank once again.

Then the phone rang.

Betty darted over to the table and picked up the receiver. I looked on as she paused and listened. She said, 'Yes. Hold on,' then passed the receiver over to me. 'For you.' Betty stood, listening intently.

'Jackie-boy?' asked Will Preston.

'Yeah.' I breathed a sigh of relief. 'Whatcha got for me, Will?'

'Who's the girl, Jack? She sounds cute.'

'That's Betty,' I said, smiling at her as I spoke. 'My secretary. And, yeah, she is.'

Betty's cheeks turned a deep pink.

'What's she like?' said Will. 'Describe her to me, man.'

'Another time, Will. Please. I'm on a case here.'

'Yeah, yeah. You're no fun, Jack. Just like the old days.'

I drummed my fingers on the little phone table, hoping that Will would get the hint.

'Okay. Your boy Fallon has been involved in a lot of minor misdemeanours out here: nothing that would attract too much attention, until recently. Apparently he's wanted in connection with the shooting of a cop – an officer Clarence Trent – in Hollywood a couple of weeks ago. I don't have any more details. That's all the local precinct boys would give me. But they want this chump bad, Jack. I'm surprised he managed to skip town in one piece.'

'And the wife?' I asked.

'Nope. Nuthin' on her.'

That was a surprise. Kitty would have attracted attention wherever she went.

'Oh, and another thing,' said Will, his deep voice crackling over the exchange. 'Pretty interesting what this Fallon used to do for a living.'

Will told me Eddie Fallon's former occupation and I nearly dropped the phone.

'Jack?'

The phone receiver trembled in my hand as I held it at the side of my face.

'You still there, Jackie-boy?'

'Yeah. Thanks, Will.' I blinked. For a second there, I was almost as many miles away as Will. 'I was just thinking. Thanks a bundle, pal. Listen, next time I see you, dinner's on me: as opposed to being on your Hawaiian shirt.'

'I'll hold you to that, Jack.'

'Give my love to Martha.'

'Will do, buddy.' There was a click and the line went dead.

As I hung up the phone, Betty looked at me expectantly, eyes wide with anticipation. 'Well?'

For the first time in what seemed like a long while, I grinned like a loon.

'What are you smilin' at, Jack? Tell me.'

'I got a plan, babe.'

'So what is it?' Betty sighed, with a hint of impatience.

I picked up the heavy, well-thumbed phone directory from its place underneath the little table. 'We're gonna find Eddie Fallon and deliver me right to him.'

Instinct told me that Eddie wouldn't leave town until he had taken his revenge on me, his wife's killer. In my favour was the fact that, as far as he was concerned, we hadn't been formally introduced. Thanks to my disguise at Earl's, he wouldn't know exactly what I looked or sounded like. And I had Betty to help me.

It took over an hour of phone calls to every hotel within a five-block radius to find out where Eddie was. And whaddya know, he was at the last place I expected him to be, and the first place we should've checked: room 604 at the Broadway Plaza. Of course he would be there, where his estranged, late wife had been staying.

Now I watched Betty as she talked on the phone to Fallon. She was nervous, but she was coping well. I'd given her a cover story and some lines to say.

She said she was a police despatch clerk who'd received the report of the whereabouts of my car, and uniforms had traced me and were about to pick me up. She spun the yarn deeper, saying that she'd tipped me off about the cops, and that I'd find someone to help me at the Broadway Plaza. And, for going to all this trouble, she told Fallon that she expected a handsome fee. And that she'd be in touch after Fallon had dealt with me.

Clear as mud, right?

Don't knock it. I was making all this up as I went along.

'One hour?' said Betty, into the telephone. 'He'll be there.' She replaced the phone receiver on its cradle and looked at me. 'He sounded horrible. His voice was so cold, like ice.'

'Sorry to put you through all that, but well done.' I consulted my watch. 'I'd better get moving. Will you be all right here on your own?'

Betty nodded. 'Take care, Jack.'

She gave me a peck on the cheek for good luck. It felt nice to have someone in this world that actually cared about me. Betty was my rock. It was about time I started to treat her better.

'Say, before I go, Toots,' I said, 'I gotta ask one last favour.'

'Name it.'

'I need to make a couple more phone calls.'

Chapter Twelve

604 revisited

I slipped the aged doorman at the Broadway Plaza 20 bucks. He looked around suspiciously, making sure the coast was clear, then nodded gratefully, stuffed the bills into his waistcoat pocket and stood aside to let me in.

The sourpuss from the previous night was on the reception desk again. I took great pleasure in ignoring her scowling face, walked right past, and headed for the lift. At least I didn't feel out of place this time, because I knew a lowlife like Eddie Fallon was now a resident.

'Hey, you!' She had a voice like nails scraping down a brick wall. 'You can't come in here! I'll call the cops!'

'Why not?' I glanced back at her as I strode into the lift. 'They'll be interested to know that you're harbouring a known criminal upstairs.'

She glared at me with cold eyes as the lift doors closed. That should keep her out of my hair for a little while. Although she was probably phoning Eddie to tell him I was on my way up. I knew he'd have someone on the lookout there. How else would he have known that I'd accompanied Kitty back to her room the previous night?

I pressed the button for the sixth floor. The lift ascended slowly, clanking noisily, before juddering to a halt on the sixth. The doors parted and I stepped into the familiar, glossy white corridor once more. I took a left, then a right turn, past the other impassive room doors. Soon I stood in front of room 604. As I rapped on the door, I felt a tightening in my gut. I stubbornly convinced myself that I could handle this.

There was the sound of a key twisting in the lock, and the door creaked open. I ventured inside, fists clenched tight, expecting to be accosted any second. The lights were dimmed low.

Sure enough, a pair of hands pulled my arms behind my back and slammed my face against the wall. Dark shapes danced across my vision, and I felt blood in my nose, dripping down onto my upper lip from my right nostril. The pair of hands quickly frisked me, patting me down and checking my pockets for weapons; and finding none. My spare piece was at the office, but I'd had enough of guns at that moment anyway. The pair of hands swung my body round roughly, and slammed my head back against the wall. I was staring into the sneering face of Eddie Fallon.

'Room service?' I said hopefully.

He cuffed me across the face with the back of his right hand.

'Hey, man. I thought I was coming here for some help.' I made a token attempt to keep to the not-very-convincing cover story from earlier. 'Is this how you help people? 'Cos I ain't impressed.'

'I nearly didn't recognise you without your mask, Wolfman.' He slapped me in the mouth.

'Bit of a change for you,' I said.

'Say what?' He held his right hand at my throat. His touch was cold, reptilian, curling round my neck like a snake.

'Hitting a man instead of a dame,' I gurgled.

'At least I draw the line at shooting them.' He backhanded me again, harder this time, cutting my lip. He loosened his grip.

I rubbed my neck, breathing heavily.

'Talking of which ...' Fallon reached inside his suit pocket and pulled out a gun.

It was a small automatic: snub nose, probably a .22 calibre. He slipped the safety off, and trained the pistol at my face. A shot at this close range would probably take my head clean off.

'Don't miss,' I said.

'You've caused me a lot of trouble, fella,' he grimaced. 'So you're Sharp – the private eye who's been sticking his nose into my business. And sticking something else into my wife.'

'We need to talk.'

'Nah. I need to kill you.'

I nodded at the gun. 'That'll make a hell of a noise.'

'Don't sweat it.' He smiled nastily. 'Not your problem.'

'I know all about your little game, Eddie.'

'That a fact?'

'Sure,' I said.

'Sounds like you're playing for time, scummo. Well, at least you won't tell anyone else.'

'How do you know I haven't already?'

He swore under his breath. 'Okay, wiseguy. Talk. While you've still got a face.' He lowered the gun, but kept the safety off. 'What do you think you know?'

I grunted, swallowing the blood in my mouth, feeling its metallic taste sliding down the back of my throat. 'I know what you've been playing at, out in LA, and here in New York.'

That rattled him. He flinched for a second, before jamming the pistol muzzle against my right cheek. The cold metal of it bored into my skin. 'Spill the beans, Sharp.'

'Not with a gun in my face,' I mumbled, barely able to move my mouth.

He withdrew the pistol a couple of inches, but kept it trained on me. Then he took me by the scruff of the neck and propelled me into the centre of the room. I stumbled forward, knocking over a vase on top of a cabinet, but not breaking it. I flailed towards the divan in the corner. I looked around. The room was much the same as when I had last seen it, except that now there was an open suitcase on the four-poster bed, with a load of clothes strewn all around. Eddie had obviously been in the middle of packing when I showed up. 'You going on vacation?' I asked.

'Siddown,' ordered Fallon. 'And I'll ask the questions.' He punched me in the stomach for good measure.

I gasped with pain and slumped back onto the divan. 'You're a real tough guy, Eddie. No wonder Kitty was desperate to get away from you.'

'You don't mention her name again.' He brought the gun up once more.

'Why not?' I snarled.

'Because you killed her,' Fallon roared, his eyes wide with fury. 'You killed my wife!'

'Oh, yeah?' I stared down the barrel of the gun. My face was defiant. Sweat on my brow and blood in my mouth. 'Why don't you just drop this damned fool charade?'

Eddie's finger hovered over the trigger. 'On your knees,' he said, motioning to the floor with the pistol. 'And keep your hands where I can see them.'

I did as I was told.

I waited for the shot that would send me to Heaven – or more likely Hell. But it didn't come.

Instead, the bathroom door opened, and a silhouette appeared in the doorframe, clothed in the dim ambience of the room. 'Wait,' said a familiar, cool voice. 'Don't kill him just yet, darling.' The figure moved closer, backlit by the glow from the lamp that shone from the centre of the ceiling above us.

Either I'd successfully played a hunch bigger than Quasimodo's, or I was looking at a ghost.

It was Kitty.

Chapter Thirteen

Explanation

'Well, well, well,' I said. 'Just as I thought. I never did believe in spooks.'

She was dressed, appropriately enough, all in black. She had on a two-piece trouser suit, tied at the waist with a belt, and a dark blouse underneath. Her golden hair was tied up in an elegant French roll. A few wisps of hair fell down behind her ears, resting upon the pale skin of her neck

'You look like you're going to a funeral,' I observed. 'Although, for a while there, I thought I was about to attend yours.'

'Looks like you'll just have to make do with your own,' grunted Fallon.

'How did you know I was still alive, Jack?' asked Kitty. She was genuinely curious.

'Who cares?' Fallon scowled. 'Let's waste him and get out of here.'

Kitty shook her head, and stepped towards me. 'Tell me, Jack. I really want to know how you figured it out.'

'Oh, I thought you were dead, all right.' I nodded towards Fallon, who was still pointing the gun at me. 'Until I found out your so-called-husband's former occupation out in Hollywood.'

Kitty moved closer. 'Go on. I know how private dicks love to tell anyone who'll listen just how clever they are.'

Fallon was itching to off me. He looked tense, angry.

I sniffed, and then dared to wipe some blood from my cut lip. 'Well, Kitty – if that actually is your real name – once I learned that Eddie here used to work on Hollywood movies, and that his particular area of expertise was guns, then it all started to fall into place.'

Kitty smiled.

Fallon grimaced. 'Keep your hands up.'

I continued, my eyes on Kitty. 'The whole diner scenario was a set-up within a set-up. When I shot you, my gun really was filled with blanks. That's why you were so determined for me to fire at you. You were perfectly safe, because Eddie rigged fake "squibs" to impact on your chest, bursting little blood bags that made it look like real bullet wounds. "Special effects", I believe it's called. Movie magic.' I glanced at Fallon. 'I gotta hand it to you, though; you did a good job. I was convinced I was a murderer.'

'Gee, thanks,' Fallon sneered, his gruff voice dripping with insincerity.

'What about you, Kitty?' I asked, although the question was a rhetorical one. 'You're an out-of-work movie extra –'

'Background artiste,' she interjected, tersely.

'Right,' I said, distracted. 'Feel free to correct me again if I'm wrong. Everyone in Hollywood wants to be a movie star. You're pretty. You've got talent. But work is slow, so you hook up with Eddie. And then what? You decide to become a couple of grifters – con artists.' My eyes narrowed as I stared at her. 'Or would that be *artistes*?'

'Shut up, Jack,' hissed Kitty.

'Oh, I'm just getting started,' I said. 'Remember when we first met, I told you I needed to know the "why"?'

'Yes.'

'Why go to all this trouble to set me up? I couldn't work it out. I thought about it for a long time. "Why?" And the only thing I could think of was this. You take out some heavy-duty life insurance policies in your name; you dupe some sap into faking your death; you lie low for a while; and Eddie, the grieving widower, cashes in the policies. Meanwhile, the patsy – me, in this particular case – goes to the chair or the chamber for your murder. I presume you then concoct a new identity, move to another state and do it all over again.' I took a breath. 'How am I doing?'

'You're doing very well,' Kitty said. She clapped her hands together gently in a little round of mock applause, then folded her arms across her chest.

Fallon rolled his eyes, impatient or bored, or maybe a mixture of both. It was difficult to tell.

'But you got sloppy,' I said. 'Out in Hollywood, you shot a cop.'

'It wasn't our fault,' protested Kitty, momentarily dropping her ice maiden mask. 'He was the patsy out in LA. But he wouldn't play ball. Instead of going along with the plan, he wanted me for himself.'

'I only meant to scare him off,' said Fallon, quietly. He lowered the pistol. 'I'm no killer.' Then, it was as if he tried to convince himself otherwise. He raised the gun again, and pointed it at me once more, a determined look on his face. 'Things change, though, man.'

I had to keep them, especially Fallon, occupied, for just a little longer. I rambled on: 'I was suspicious from the moment I met you, Kitty.'

'How come?'

'Remember I asked if you'd ever been to The Alley Cat nightclub in LA, and you said you had?'

'Uh-huh.'

'There's no such place,' I replied. ''Course, clients rarely tell the whole truth, they tell you just enough to get you interested in their particular case; but it made me wary right from the start.'

'Clever, Jack.' Kitty walked around the room, as cool as ever.

'As for you, Eddie,' I said. 'I pretty much believed Kitty's story, that you were a heel who beat up on her. But there was one thing that niggled away at me about you, like an itch I couldn't scratch. I realised what it was eventually, though.'

'Don't keep us in suspense, man,' said a sarcastic Fallon.

'It was when you paid two goons off the sidewalk to give me a going over. A real, big shot crime boss would've brought his own personal security with him. He'd never trust local muscle.'

'Well deduced, Sherlock,' growled Fallon. 'Pity you're not gonna be around to pat yourself on the back.'

Kitty ignored her partner's feeble attempt at tough talk. 'Well, obviously, we didn't want you to realise that Eddie and I were playing you. And we didn't want you two to meet at that point. We had to make it look like Eddie was the kind of guy who would intimidate a poor defenceless dame like little old me.' She let out a mocking laugh. 'And you would be my knight in shining armour, Jack. And you know what? You fell for it, hook, line and sinker. Like the big, greedy, horny dope that I took you for the moment I strolled into your office. Grifting's just like being at grade school, Mr Sharp. We'd done our homework. You were the mark most likely to go along with our plan. An old-fashioned, chivalrous lunkhead, desperate for money.'

'You might have to work on that whole "flattery" thing,' I said. 'You don't seem to have quite got the hang of it just yet.'

'Well, what did you expect?' retorted Kitty.

'I didn't expect to fall in love with you, Kitty.' My voice was solemn.

For the first time since I'd met her, two long days before, Kitty looked like she was at a loss for words. She opened her beautiful, cruel mouth to speak, but no sound came out.

My last comment had riled Fallon. He took a step closer and levelled the pistol at the side of my head. 'Guess what? I decided that I am a killer after all.'

I saw him look at Kitty, like a little boy looking for approval from his mommy.

She nodded, her face emotionless.

Using his left hand, Fallon pulled the slide on the automatic, putting a round into the breech. A tiny click reverberated in my ear, amplified a thousand-fold, as loud as the clock in Grand Central Station as it struck 12. Sticking with the clock analogy, I was out of time.

He really was gonna execute me.

Chapter Fourteen

Altercation

'Go ahead,' I said. 'Add to your growing list of crimes, why don't ya? Real smart. Gold star, Eddie.'

'He's playing for time,' said Kitty, her mouth barely moving. 'Plug him. Now.'

'Congrats. Your first real murder. No doubt the first of many, but the first is always the worst. Believe me, I know these things. It'll mess with your head, make you sick; haunt you forever.'

I was warming to my subject. Note to self: I gotta write this stuff down.

'You'll wake up in a cold sweat in the middle of the night. playing over and over again the moment where you splatter my brains across the wall like a ripe melon.'

'I'm sure he'll get over it,' Kitty said.

'I made a couple of calls before I came here. One was to the Coroner's office. I was looking to chat to Ritchie Vine – your "cousin" who was gonna oblige you with a death certificate. No-one there by that name. What a surprise.'

'Of course there was no cousin,' said Kitty. 'We wanted that to sound simple enough for you not to actually bother checking up on it.' She grinned. 'And I knew I'd be able to keep you occupied the evening before the scam.'

'You still need a death certificate, and presumably a body, to get your insurance claim,' I said, thinking aloud. 'So I guess you'll grease a few palms at the Coroner's to do that. Am I right?'

'Top of the class.'

'And after all,' I sneered, 'who could resist someone like you?'

'Enough yakking,' said Kitty.

'I know. I'm almost getting tired of my own voice here too. But I didn't tell you about my other phone call.'

'Spill it,' Fallon growled.

'The boys in blue are on their way. In fact, they're probably standing outside the door right now, arguing about who gets to kick it in this time. I'm sure they'll be more than happy to arrest you for Murder One, as well as fraud. If they don't blow you both away first, that is.'

'You talk too much,' grimaced Kitty.

I kept yapping like an old lady at a hair salon. 'Oh yeah. I got one last newsflash for ya, tough guy. I called in a few favours and found out from LAPD that the cop you winged is gonna pull through.'

'Kill him!' Kitty's voice screeched.

'Shut up, both of you!' screamed Fallon. His eyes were staring, pupils black and dilated like those of a man in a fever. A sheen of clammy sweat glistened on his forehead. The gun trembled in his right hand. He clasped his left hand against it, trying to steady his grip on the weapon. He glanced round at Kitty, blinking in confusion.

This was my last chance to live.

I propelled myself up off my knees, launching my body at Fallon like a greyhound out of the trap. I hit him with all the force of a freight train, pushing him backwards. He reeled, arms flailing like a comedy drunk.

The gun went off.

The muzzle flash blinded me, white light flashed across my vision for a split second. The shot rang in my ears for a lot longer. I was deafened. I had nothing but hissing in my ears, like a swimmer who's just surfaced from underwater. The pungent reek of cordite and sulphur filled my nostrils, making me want to retch.

I was lucky. I hadn't been shot. Yet.

A cloud of dark gun-smoke hung in the air, stinging my already raw eyelids. The smoke dissipated enough for me to see that Fallon wasn't hit either. I reached out, grabbing at him. I struggled to disarm him, desperately trying to wrestle the gun from his grasp. He lashed out with his left hand and caught me with a lucky punch to the side of the head. Yet more pain. He and I plunged to the floor in a tangled heap of arms and legs. Fallon dropped the gun. It bounced across the carpet. We both scrabbled around for it. He got lucky once again, managing to claw the pistol back into his grip. He pulled the gun up in front of him, barely having time to aim. He squeezed the trigger and another loud shot rang out, wreathing us in another mist of gun-smoke that wrenched at our lungs, causing us to cough and choke.

Again I hadn't been hit. A miracle. Somebody up there must like Jack Sharp. Either that or somebody down below is in no hurry to meet me just yet.

This was getting like a schoolyard scuffle, except much more dangerous, and there was more than my lunch money at stake.

I dazedly blinked around the smoky room. Kitty was at the main door, fumbling with the key in the lock, trying to prise it open. She was going to get away.

Time to end this.

Time to fight dirty.

Sure, I'm a big guy who's a little outta shape, but I can move fast when I want to. Three years on the high school football team does that to a man. In a last burst of nervous energy, I dropped to the floor and swung my leg round in a tight arc, catching Fallon in the right kneecap with my foot. He cried out in pain, dropping the gun, which fell downwards with a dull thud. I kicked the gun across the carpeted floor. I moved fast, leaping in front of him. He was probably expecting me to try a punch. So I grabbed both his nipples through his shirt and squeezed them tight like I was turning the volume control up full on a radio. He shrieked in pain. I poked him in the left eye with an extended forefinger. They wanted a stooge? So I gave them three for the price of one. I planted a fist into the grifter's stomach. He gasped for breath, pitching forwards onto his damaged knee, and then howled in agony. I socked him with one last right hook to the jaw. His head crashed against the side of the coffee table. Then Fallon went down face first like a sack of potatoes, and lay still. Like I said, three years on the high school football team really does teach you a thing or two.

I rubbed my raw-red knuckles and said grimly: 'And you're out.'

Kitty was still struggling at the door in vain. 'Open, damn you!' she screamed.

I could hear raised voices echoing along the corridor and the rumble of approaching footsteps outside.

I knelt down, scooped up the fallen automatic and levelled it at her back. 'Get away from the door, Kitty,' I said. 'It's over.'

She whirled round. Her once-beautiful face looked twisted and evil as she stared at the gun, her blue eyes seething with rage and despair. 'You already killed me once, Jack. You man enough to do it again?'

'Don't tempt me, Kitty,' I said. 'No blanks this time.'

'You won't do it. You're weak. A spineless, overgrown schoolboy who thinks he's a tough man. Just like she said.'

Kitty's words stung like cheap cologne on a fresh shaving cut. But she wouldn't manipulate me ever again.

'Wanna bet?' I growled.

'*Police!*' roared a voice in the hallway outside. 'We're coming in!'

I lowered the gun with a sigh, and let it drop to the floor in front of me. 'Killing you once was bad enough, Kitty. Like I said; it's over.'

Chapter Fifteen

Small potatoes

There was a loud crash and a splintering of wood as the door to room 604 was kicked in and four men trampled over it. Three of them were dressed in the usual deep blue uniforms and peaked caps of the NYPD. The other guy was wearing a brown sports jacket with black pads at the elbows – the kind that tries hard to be low-key but somehow looks suspicious, and is so tasteless that only Homicide detectives wear it. They were all armed with police issue revolvers, held in front of them.

One cop searched the bathroom. 'Clear,' he said.

The other holstered his weapon and bent down to examine Fallon. 'This one's unconscious,' was his acute, if extremely obvious, conclusion.

'Nobody move! Hands up,' said the third cop, prodding his gun muzzle into my chest.

'This day keeps getting better and better.' I raised my hands for what seemed like the hundredth time that evening. I motioned with my eyes for Kitty, who was standing opposite me, to do the same.

I spoke to the one with the sports jacket. 'What the hell took you so long? Your boys stop off for a picnic on the way?'

'____ you, Sharp,' said Detective Lieutenant Frank Garfield. 'I figured you could handle things just fine an' dandy here on your own until we got here.' He rummaged around his jacket inside pocket, found a fountain pen and bent down, using it to pick up Fallon's automatic by the trigger mechanism, making sure he didn't get his prints on it.

'I appreciate the concern,' I said coldly. 'Careful; the safety's off.'

'Thanks,' said the gruff policeman. He had a tousled mop of thick, dark hair – which, surprisingly, had only recently started to grey around the temples – counterpointed by a neatly-trimmed moustache. I guessed he was aged around 45 now, but his craggy, lined face betrayed him. The permanently weary expression made him look a lot older. His dull grey eyes were red-rimmed, with dark bags hanging underneath. His nose was red and pockmarked, his lips ashen, and he had big ears with wisps of fine hair that coiled out of them.

If there ever was an argument against police officers being allowed to dress in plain clothes, then Garfield was it. He had on a light blue shirt with white collar. A hideous, purple-coloured satin knot, that had presumably once resembled a tie, complemented the muddy brown corduroy sports jacket. Or, more accurately, didn't complement it, if you get my meaning. This crime against good taste was completed with dark pants and brown leather loafers.

He found a small, plastic evidence bag in another pocket, and popped the pistol inside. Then, pointing the gun away from everyone in the room, he clicked the safety catch back into place.

The second cop was trying to revive Fallon. He sat the hapless grifter up against the side of the bed and slapped him across the cheek, gently at first, then harder. 'Wake up, bozo,' the flatfoot whined.

'Mind telling me what the ____'s going on here, Sharp?' demanded Garfield.

'This man was about to attack me, sir,' Kitty butted in. Her voice was deliberately high-pitched and hysterical. The foul-mouthed detective turned to Kitty and pointed a warning forefinger in her face. 'I wasn't talking to you, Blondie.'

'Charming.' Kitty tutted, and fell into a moody silence.

Garfield growled in my direction once more. 'Tell me a story. And make it a good one.'

'These two lowlifes framed me for the robbery at Earl's Diner earlier today.'

'Keep talkin',' rumbled Garfield.

'They set me up. Tried to implicate me in her so-called murder. It's kind of a long story, Frank.'

'I'm all ears.'

I managed not to scoff at that remark.

Garfield's back up officers were obviously used to him saying that by now. None of them even flinched. Admirable.

'A scam?' asked Garfield.

'Yeah,' I admitted. I scratched at the back of my neck with my right hand, feeling kinda awkward. 'And they duped me like a rookie on his first day on the beat.'

'You brought me across town for a dumb con-job like this? Still, it does explain why I had a murder scene with no ____ing corpse.' Garfield's voice was incredulous. 'Small potatoes, Sharp.' He shook his head, almost like he was disappointed in me. 'You always were.'

Who did he think he was, my dad?

I said: 'They're also responsible for a cop shooting out in Hollywood.'

'Yeah, yeah. So you said earlier when you were bending my ear over the phone.'

'So I caught them for ya.' The words hissed impatiently out of the side of my mouth. I was starting to get riled up again. I needed to calm down.

'Don't get me wrong, Sharp. I appreciate what you've done here,' said Garfield. 'But you're lucky I don't arrest you as a ____ing accessory!'

'That's a funny way to say "thanks", Frank,' I grimaced.

There was a low groan from the side of the bed in the corner. Fallon stirred, looking around at the six people in the room with a confused frown on his face. An ugly red mark was already forming on his jaw from when I'd socked him. He groggily got to his feet. His bewildered gaze eventually settled on Kitty. 'Wh-what's going on, honey?'

Kitty opened her mouth to speak, but Garfield cut her off. He nodded to the whiny cop. 'Cuff him.'

'Yes, sir.' The cop grabbed Fallon by his shoulders and turned the delirious grifter round, putting his hands behind his back and fastening a pair of cuffs round his wrists.

'You can't do this,' protested Fallon. 'I'm a businessman from LA, in town on important business. Get out of my room now, all of you!'

I grinned. The whack I'd given Fallon earlier now had him really believing his cover story. 'Looks like you'll be swapping your room for a slightly cheaper one.'

'Huh?' grunted Fallon.

'Four-poster bed, en suite bathroom, panoramic view of the city ... None of that where you're going,' I smirked. 'More like a ten by eight with two square meals a day. I hope you like bread and

84

water.'

'What?' he cried, squirming like a worm on a fishhook. 'I demand to speak to a lawyer!'

'We'll be only too happy to oblige,' said Garfield. 'Downtown.' He nodded towards Kitty, saying, 'Cuff her as well.'

'___ you, ' growled Kitty. 'This ain't fair!' Her pretty face was now twisted in a grotesque parody of the woman she had once been. Or, rather, the woman she had recently *played*. She was an actress, after all.

One of the other officers, the tall one with fair hair, got his set of cuffs ready. 'Hands behind your back, Miss.'

'___ you too!' She lashed out at the cop with her right hand, tearing at the side of his face. Her nails scratched at his cheek, leaving three small, scarlet slashes where the skin had broken.

The cop recoiled and put a hand to his face. 'Aah!' His cuffs thumped to the carpeted floor.

I sprang forward and caught Kitty's wrists. 'Stop it,' I hissed, my face inches from hers. 'You're only making things worse for yourself.'

'Don't you touch me!' she screamed. 'I swear I'll kill you!'

I kept hold of her wrists. She struggled with all her might. Then she spat in my face. I looked in disgust at this snarling, spitting harpy in front of me. Was this the real Kitty?

'I don't know you,' I said, wiping her saliva from my face. 'I don't know you at all.'

She gave me a look of pure hatred, glinting in her eyes like jagged flashes of lightning in a granite sky.

Garfield scowled and signalled to the whiny cop. He picked up the fallen cuffs, clicked them open and forced them round Kitty's exposed wrists.

Then her wild expression lifted, as if it had been wiped from her face, like a window cleaner using a chamois on a dirty pane. Perhaps she'd realised that she finally had to stop playing a part; although, for Kitty, that could never be.

In a monotonous tone, Garfield started to read Kitty her rights. But she ignored him and turned to me.

'Jack,' she whispered, her voice low and desperate. In fact, her voice was different. The practised, husky tone had disappeared, replaced with a Midwest drawl. 'What'll happen to me now?'

'You'll probably be sent back to LA jurisdiction for trial.'

'But I don't wanna go back. I can't go back.'

'Nothin' to do with us,' retorted an increasingly impatient Garfield.

'You've gotta help me, Jack. You're the only who can'.

Kitty had really gotten under my skin. I had almost committed crimes for her. She was like a virus, corrupting my mind, my body and my soul. I knew that I had to get rid of that virus before it killed me.

I shook my head. 'No chance.'

'Please,' she said. 'You can't abandon me. Not after everything we shared.'

'You shared my bed, sugar,' I lied. 'Lotsa girls have done that. Wanna tell me what makes you any different from the rest of them?'

'Jack!' she implored me. She nodded towards Fallon, who was being led out of the room. 'I had it all worked out. Once the dust had settled, I was gonna ditch that stiff and come back for you. I love you. You gotta believe me!'

Once again I shook my head.

Garfield said, 'Are we done with this pantomime yet?'

'We're done.'

'No!' screamed Kitty. 'Jack, don't do this. I'm begging you!'

The cops started to drag her from the room. She dug her heels into the carpet, trying her best to stop the inevitable.

'You've lied so much, Kitty, you don't know when to stop.'

'Jack …' Her voice trailed off.

That was the last time I ever heard it.

I was left alone in the empty hotel room with Lieutenant Garfield. 'Well, Frank, I dunno who's gonna pay the room tariff, but it sure ain't gonna be me.'

'You're lucky you ain't being dragged kicking and screaming out of here with those two.'

'I know,' I admitted. 'Thanks.'

'What the ____ do you think this is, Jack?' drawled Garfield. 'Christmas?'

'Well, you ain't Santa Claus. I know that,' I replied.

Garfield rummaged in his sports jacket pocket and brought out another plastic evidence bag. My .38 was in it, a white evidence tag hanging from the trigger. 'I wanted to make sure of your side of the story first,' explained Garfield. 'It's filled with one blank and five empty casings, so I guess that means you're telling the truth.'

'Hey, maybe you really are Santa Claus,' I said, relieved. 'You ain't as mean as you like to make out.'

'Don't tell nobody. Or I'll hafta kill you,' he said, his voice laconic.

I stepped forward to take the gun back.

Garfield shook his head. 'Uh-uh. This stays with me for now, hotshot.'

'Sure,' I nodded. 'Fair enough.'

'You'll need to report to the DA's office, pronto. That means first thing tomorrow morning.'

'I'm tired, Frank,' I sighed. 'How does first thing in the afternoon sound?'

'Sounds exactly like something your average private eye would say. And they don't get much more average than you. With that kind of attitude, how do you guys ever make any money?'

'With great difficulty,' I agreed. 'But, going by my usual standards, this case has been a success.'

Garfield frowned. 'And what are your usual standards, exactly? I'm curious.'

'Nobody died,' I said. 'Me, in particular. Dead bodies are bad for business.'

I put a finger to my tender, bust lip. Some dried blood had crusted there. My face throbbed like a traffic beacon.

'Looks like you've gone 15 rounds with Marciano,' said Garfield. 'Say, you own a beige Buick?'

'Yeah.'

'One was towed into the vehicle pound this afternoon. It was almost as beat up as you. You can pay to get it back tomorrow.' He nodded towards the splintered door. 'I'll clear things up here.'

'You're letting me go?'

'Yeah. Well deduced, Jack. Now get outta here before I change my mind. I must be getting soft in my old age.'

'You're all right, Frank,' I replied. 'See you around.'

'I sincerely hope not.' He gave me a lopsided grin.

I stepped through the remains of the doorframe and into the corridor.

A uniformed cop and an oily, obsequious looking man, who I presumed was the hotel manager, were trying to calm down a handful of angry residents milling around and muttering outside their room doors.

I pushed past an elderly couple doddering around the landing in their complimentary, matching fluffy white dressing gowns. I caught the lift and descended to ground level. The reception area was full of people too. As I came into the main lobby, I saw with some satisfaction that the sourpuss receptionist from earlier was in a blazing row with another uniformed police officer. The crusty doorman I'd bribed on the way in was distracted by all the noise, so I left quietly.

Just as I had a couple of nights before – was it really that short a time? – I felt like walking.

I strode through the quiet streets, amazed that I had actually lived through this case. It had been a slippy situation and no mistake, slippier than a snake in a barrel full of baby oil.

Loverboy Fallon would probably end up in San Q.

And Kitty?

I wasn't sure. She'd probably put on a show for whatever foolhardy lawyer took on her case, and convince him that she'd only been following the orders of her cruel conman of a husband. She'd also end up in jail, that was for sure. I had no doubt whatsoever that she'd make lots of new friends in the LA State Pen.

Kitty had tried to give me the Long, Big Kiss Goodbye. And she had very nearly succeeded. If ever a Kitty had nine lives, I mused, then she had lost one of them.

I automatically patted my coat pockets for cigarettes, just like I always did, and found only an empty pack. I crumpled it up and threw it in the gutter. Ah, what the hell.

Maybe it was time to quit once and for all.

Chapter Sixteen

The morning after

My meeting with the DA was scheduled for 11.30. I had plenty of time to swing by the office and check that everything was okay. And I had some important work to do, which wouldn't take long.

I brought out my keys and opened up. I crouched down, ignoring the dull ache of my sore leg, and picked up the handful of mail that lay on the inside mat. No doubt there were some fascinating additions to my ever burgeoning, prized collections of unpaid invoices and parking tickets among it. Financially, I was a joke. I didn't have a dime to my name, and I barely brought in enough green to pay the rent on the place. At that moment, money was tighter than a showgirl's corset. I tried to convince myself that something would come up soon.

The office stank of stale cigarette smoke and sweat. I went over to the window, pulled the string that drew up the Venetian blinds and pushed the heavy window frame upwards. Fresh air flooded into the dank office, ruffling my hair and filling my nostrils. Early morning traffic buzzed around the streets below, and already the car horns and police sirens had started.

I set to work.

About half an hour later there was the sound of a key scraping in the main door lock, and then the door itself swung open with a creak, when the person on the outside realised that it was already unlocked.

Betty was standing in the doorway. She was wearing a navy blue jacket and matching knee-length skirt, with a cream coloured blouse underneath the jacket. Her brown curls were tied back in a loose bun, and she wasn't wearing her spectacles.

'Jack!' she exclaimed in surprise. 'Thank goodness you're all right. Why didn't you call me last night to say you were okay? I was worried sick, ya big lunk!'

I was sitting behind her desk, in her seat. She rushed over, stooping down to embrace me.

I gently withdrew from her grasp, and looked up into her brown eyes. 'Bet you weren't expecting to see me, huh? Especially at this time in the morning.'

'Yeah!' she said, in a high-pitched, excited squeal. 'So what happened last night? Tell me everything –' Betty's words were cut short when she looked at her desk, noticing that all her personal stuff was packed into a large cardboard box. Some books, and the treasured photograph of her Mom, were visible under the lid. 'What's goin' on, Jack?'

'I cleared out your desk.'

Betty's face turned ashen grey. 'Why? Whatcha do that for?'

''Cos you're fired.'

'What?' she said, incredulously. 'Why?'

'You sold me out to Kitty and Fallon, Betty. And you almost got away with it.'

'Are you out of your mind?' she said, gazing at me with what she no doubt hoped were shocked, disbelieving eyes. 'I'd never do such a thing!'

'Quit while you're ahead,' I said, softly. 'You're nowhere near as good an actress as Kitty.'

As soon as I spoke her name, I pictured Kitty from the night before, her image replaying in my head like a cinema newsreel:

'You're weak. A spineless, overgrown schoolboy who thinks he's a tough man. *Just like she said.*'

I got up from behind Betty's desk and walked towards her. I asked gently: 'Why'd you do it?'

She was silent. She didn't look at me, preferring instead to stare towards the window.

'Answer me, dammit!' I snarled, anger surging through my veins. 'You were the one person I could rely on. The one thing in my crummy life that sparkled. You always kept me out of the gutter,

Betty. But maybe I belong there.' My voice quivered with emotion. 'Why?' I repeated, more forceful this time.

Betty's shoulders jerked upwards, momentarily startled by the fury in my voice.

'Because I love you,' she whispered. Then she turned round, glaring at me with burning eyes. 'And I hate you too!'

'It's usually one or the other, Toots,' I sneered.

'I wanted you to know what it felt like to be hurt,' she said, quietly. 'Just the way you've hurt me. For as long as I could remember, I'd put up with all those other women you'd lusted after – hoping that one day you would realise what you had right under your nose. I just wanted you to want *me*. But you never did. I couldn't take it any more!' She buried her face in her hands, starting to sob quietly.

'So what happened?' I asked. 'Did Kitty come to you, looking for a patsy, saying she'd cut you in on the deal?'

Betty looked up, tears misting her eyes. 'It was the guy, Fallon. He said I'd get a share of any profit they made from the insurance pay out.' She sniffed. 'But I didn't care about the money, Jack.'

'You expect me to believe that?'

'It's true,' she said, adamantly. 'I was hoping that you'd be able to figure it all out, and stop them, and then you'd –'

'– Come running to you in my hour of need,' I cut in. 'Just like I did. Smart thinking, Betty.'

I'd been played more times than a gramophone record these past few nights, and now I was sick of being such a sap.

'When did you realise it was me?' asked Betty. She wiped at a bead of sweat on her forehead with the back of her right hand.

'I didn't,' I replied. 'Not at first. It only struck me later how easily you let me off the hook for... y'know ...' My voice kinda tailed off there.

'Sleeping with that double-crossing bitch.' Betty finished the sentence for me. Somewhat hypocritically, I have to say. Although, let's face it, if we were talking hypocrites here... I quickly changed the subject:

'If Kitty and Fallon had kept their side of the deal, you'd have had the beginnings of a nice little bundle to keep safe for a rainy day,' I said. 'And it always rains in New York.'

'Jack –'

I carried on talking, thinking aloud more than anything. 'Even if I hadn't escaped from the diner, then I would have been out of your hair for good: in prison, or in a wooden overcoat. Either way, you would have won.'

'I know it seems a crazy way to go about things,' said Betty.

'But I did it for *us.*'

'You did it for *you,*' I replied, coldly. 'The thing is, you were so close to getting exactly what you wanted. Last night, I was all set to ask you become a partner in the business, and to move in with me. Maybe even get hitched.'

'But, we can still do that,' she said, her face hopeful. 'Please, Jack. We can put all this behind us.'

I shook my head. 'I'm sorry about the way I treated you, Betty. I know I ain't exactly been a saint these past coupla years. But I can't let this go.'

'Sure you can,' said Betty. She leaned towards me, trying to take my arm in hers.

'No.' I shrugged her away, even though it pained me to do it.

Tears cascaded down Betty's cheeks, smudging her make-up. 'Please, Jack,' she said again.

'Just take your stuff and go,' I said, nodding towards the box on the desk. 'As far as I know, the cops don't know you're involved. I won't tell them anything. I'll say that you got another job some place, if they ever come looking for you.'

'Jack. I don't wanna –'

'Just go, Betty!' I strode towards the main door, grappled with the handle, and held it open.

Without another word, Betty gathered the box up into her arms, then walked out of the door, and out of my life.

I heard the *ping* of the lift in the hallway outside. I left the door open, to let more fresh air into the stuffy office.

I stood at the window, gazing out onto the streets below, wondering if I'd just made the biggest mistake of my life.

I longed for a cigarette. I took a deep breath. And smelt the sweet, mesmerising scent of perfume.

I turned round.

Standing in front of me was a dame. A beautiful dame. One I'd never seen before. And I never forget a face, especially one as pretty as this. Something had just come up.

But that's another story. Remind me to tell you sometime.

ACKNOWLEDGEMENTS

Sincere thanks to Steve Walker and David Howe at Telos Publishing, and to Dan McGachey for casting an eye over the manuscript and coming up with some excellent suggestions. Thanks also to my family, and to all my friends and colleagues for their encouragement and support during the writing of this book. Finally, there's a special mention for my wife, Annette: for her patience and understanding, and for putting up with me.

ABOUT THE AUTHOR

Scott Montgomery's written work has appeared in many publications, including: *Judge Dredd Megazine*, *2000AD*, *Comics International*, *Dreamwatch*, *Starburst*, *Cult Times*, *Shivers* and *Doctor Who Magazine*. He has also written for several other titles, such as the *Sunday Mail*, *The List – Glasgow & Edinburgh Events Guide* and *The Big Issue*.

He was a full-time sub-editor on *The Dandy* for two years, writing hundreds of weekly comic scripts for this long-running children's title, published by DC Thomson & Co Ltd. He is now assistant editor of *Commando* comic books for the same company.

He is also a regular contributor to *Watson's Wind Up* – BBC Radio Scotland's topical, weekly comedy show, starring Jonathan Watson.

Scott was born in Glasgow in 1972, and now lives in Dundee, Scotland.

The Long, Big Kiss Goodbye is his first book.

Other Telos Titles Available

TIME HUNTER

A range of high-quality, original paperback and limited edition hardback novellas featuring the adventures in time of Honoré Lechasseur. Part mystery, part detective story, part dark fantasy, part science fiction … these books are guaranteed to enthral fans of good fiction everywhere, and are in the spirit of our acclaimed range of *Doctor Who* Novellas.

THE WINNING SIDE by LANCE PARKIN
Emily is dead! Killed by an unknown assailant. Honoré and Emily find themselves caught up in a plot reaching from the future to their past, and with their very existence, not to mention the future of the entire world, at stake, can they unravel the mystery before it is too late?
An adventure in time and space.
£7.99 (+ £1.50 UK p&p) Standard p/b ISBN 1-903889-35-9 (pb)

THE TUNNEL AT THE END OF THE LIGHT
by STEFAN PETRUCHA
In the heart of post-war London, a bomb is discovered lodged at a disused station between Green Park and Hyde Park Corner. The bomb detonates, and as the dust clears, it becomes apparent that *something* has been awakened. Strange half-human creatures attack the workers at the site, hungrily searching for anything containing sugar …
Meanwhile, Honoré and Emily are contacted by eccentric poet Randolph Crest, who believes himself to be the target of these subterranean creatures. The ensuing investigation brings Honoré and Emily up against a terrifying force from deep beneath the earth, and one which even with their combined powers, they may have trouble stopping.
An adventure in time and space.
£7.99 (+ £1.50 UK p&p) Standard p/b ISBN 1-903889-37-5 (pb)
£25.00 (+ £1.50 UK p&p) Deluxe h/b ISBN 1-903889-38-3 (hb)

THE CLOCKWORK WOMAN by CLAIRE BOTT

Honoré and Emily find themselves imprisoned in the 19th Century by a celebrated inventor … but help comes from an unexpected source – a humanoid automaton created by and to give pleasure to its owner. As the trio escape to London, they are unprepared for what awaits them, and at every turn it seems impossible to avert what fate may have in store for the Clockwork Woman.

An adventure in time and space.

£7.99 (+ £1.50 UK p&p) Standard p/b ISBN 1-903889-39-1 (pb)
£25.00 (+ £1.50 UK p&p) Deluxe h/b ISBN 1-903889-40-5 (hb)

KITSUNE by JOHN PAUL CATTON

In the year 2020, Honoré and Emily find themselves thrown into a mystery, as an ice spirit – *Yuki-Onna* – wreaks havoc during the Kyoto Festival, and a haunted funhouse proves to contain more than just paper lanterns and wax dummies. But what does all this have to do with the elegant owner of the Hide and Chic fashion chain … and to the legendary Chinese fox-spirits, the Kitsune?

An adventure in time and space.

£7.99 (+ £1.50 UK p&p) Standard p/b ISBN 1-903889-41-3 (pb)
£25.00 (+ £1.50 UK p&p) Deluxe h/b ISBN 1-903889-42-1 (hb)

THE SEVERED MAN by GEORGE MANN

What links a clutch of sinister murders in Victorian London, an angel appearing in a Staffordshire village in the 1920s and a small boy running loose around the capital in 1950? When Honoré and Emily encounter a man who appears to have been cut out of time, they think they have the answer. But soon enough they discover that the mystery is only just beginning and that nightmares can turn into reality.

An adventure in time and space.

£7.99 (+ £1.50 UK p&p) Standard p/b ISBN 1-903889-43-X (pb)
£25.00 (+ £1.50 UK p&p) Deluxe h/b ISBN 1-903889-44-8 (hb)

ECHOES by IAIN MCLAUGHLIN & CLAIRE BARTLETT
Echoes of the past … echoes of the future. Honoré Lechasseur can see the threads that bind the two together, however when he and Emily Blandish find themselves outside the imposing tower-block headquarters of Dragon Industry, both can sense something is wrong. There are ghosts in the building, and images and echoes of all times pervade the structure. But what is behind this massive contradiction in time, and can Honoré and Emily figure it out before they become trapped themselves … ?
An adventure in time and space.
£7.99 (+ £1.50 UK p&p) Standard p/b ISBN 1-903889-45-6 (pb)
£25.00 (+ £1.50 UK p&p) Deluxe h/b ISBN 1-903889-46-4 (hb)

PECULIAR LIVES by PHILIP PURSER-HALLARD
Once a celebrated author of 'scientific romances', Erik Clevedon is an old man now. But his fiction conceals a dangerous truth, as Honoré Lechasseur and Emily Blandish discover after a chance encounter with a strangely gifted young pickpocket. Born between the Wars, the superhuman children known as 'the Peculiar' are reaching adulthood – and they believe that humanity is making a poor job of looking after the world they plan to inherit …
An adventure in time and space.
£7.99 (+ £1.50 UK p&p) Standard p/b ISBN 1-903889-47-2 (pb)
£25.00 (+ £1.50 UK p&p) Deluxe h/b ISBN 1-903889-48-0 (hb)

DEUS LE VOLT by JON DE BURGH MILLER
'Deus Le Volt!'…'God Wills It!' The cry of the first Crusade in 1098, despatched by Pope Urban to free Jerusalem from the Turks. Honoré and Emily are plunged into the middle of the conflict on the trail of what appears to be a time travelling knight. As the siege of Antioch draws to a close, so death haunts the blood-soaked streets … and the Fendahl – a creature that feeds on life itself – is summoned. Honoré and Emily find themselves facing angels and demons in a battle to survive their latest adventure.
An adventure in time and space.
£7.99 (+ £1.50 UK p&p) Standard p/b ISBN 1-903889-49-9 (pb)
£25.00 (+ £1.50 UK p&p) Deluxe h/b ISBN 1-903889-97-9 (hb)

THE ALBINO'S DANCER by DALE SMITH

'Goodbye, little Emily.'

April 1938, and a shadowy figure attends an impromptu burial in Shoreditch, London. His name is Honoré Lechasseur. After a chance encounter with the mysterious Catherine Howkins, he's had advance warning that his friend Emily Blandish was going to die. But is forewarned necessarily forearmed? And just how far is he willing to go to save Emily's life?

Because Honoré isn't the only person taking an interest in Emily Blandish – she's come to the attention of the Albino, one of the new breed of gangsters surfacing in post-rationing London. And the only life he cares about is his own.

An adventure in time and space.

£7.99 (+ £1.50 UK p&p) Standard p/b ISBN 1-84583-100-4 (pb)
£25.00 (+ £1.50 UK p&p) Deluxe h/b ISBN 1-84583-101-2 (hb)

THE SIDEWAYS DOOR by R J CARTER & TROY RISER

Honoré and Emily find themselves in a parallel timestream where their alternate selves think nothing of changing history to improve the quality of life – especially their own. Honoré has been recently haunted by the death of his mother, an event which happened in his childhood, but now there seems to be a way to reverse that event … but at what cost? When faced with two of the most dangerous people they have ever encountered, Honoré and Emily must make some decisions with far-reaching consequences.

An adventure in time and space.

£7.99 (+ £1.50 UK p&p) Standard p/b ISBN 1-84583-102-0 (pb)
£25.00 (+ £1.50 UK p&p) Deluxe h/b ISBN 1-84583-103-9 (hb)

TIME HUNTER FILM

DAEMOS RISING
by DAVID J HOWE, DIRECTED BY KEITH BARNFATHER
Daemos Rising is a sequel to both the *Doctor Who* adventure *The Daemons* and to *Downtime*, an earlier drama featuring the Yeti. It is also a prequel of sorts to Telos Publishing's *Time Hunter* series. It stars Miles Richardson as ex-UNIT operative Douglas Cavendish, and Beverley Cressman as Brigadier Lethbridge-Stewart's daughter Kate. Trapped in an isolated cottage, Cavendish thinks he is seeing ghosts. The only person who might understand and help is Kate Lethbridge-Stewart … but when she arrives, she realises that Cavendish is key in a plot to summon the Daemons back to the Earth. With time running out, Kate discovers that sometimes even the familiar can turn out to be your worst nightmare. Also starring Andrew Wisher, and featuring Ian Richardson as the Narrator.
An adventure in time and space.
£14.00 (+ £2.50 UK p&p) PAL format R4 DVD
Order direct from Reeltime Pictures, PO Box 23435, London SE26 5WU

HORROR/FANTASY

CAPE WRATH by PAUL FINCH
Death and horror on a deserted Scottish island as an ancient Viking
warrior chief returns to life.
£8.00 (+ £1.50 UK p&p) Standard p/b ISBN: 1-903889-60-X

KING OF ALL THE DEAD by STEVE LOCKLEY & PAUL
LEWIS
The king of all the dead will have what is his.
£8.00 (+ £1.50 UK p&p) Standard p/b ISBN: 1-903889-61-8

ASPECTS OF A PSYCHOPATH by ALASTAIR LANGSTON
The twisted diary of a serial killer.
£8.00 (+ £1.50 UK p&p) Standard p/b ISBN: 1-903889-63-4

GUARDIAN ANGEL by STEPHANIE BEDWELL-GRIME
Devilish fun as Guardian Angel Porsche Winter loses a soul to the
devil …
£9.99 (+ £2.50 UK p&p) Standard p/b ISBN: 1-903889-62-6

FALLEN ANGEL by STEPHANIE BEDWELL-GRIME
Porsche Winter battles She-Devils on Earth …
£9.99 (+ £2.50 UK p&p) Standard p/b ISBN: 1-903889-69-3

SPECTRE by STEPHEN LAWS
The inseparable Byker Chapter: six boys, one girl, growing up
together in the back streets of Newcastle. Now memories are all
that Richard Eden has left, and one treasured photograph. But
suddenly, inexplicably, the images of his companions start to fade,
and as they vanish, so his friends are found dead and mutilated.
Something is stalking the Chapter, picking them off one by one,
something connected with their past, and with the girl they used to
know.
£9.99 (+ £2.50 UK p&p) Standard p/b ISBN: 1-903889-72-3

THE HUMAN ABSTRACT by GEORGE MANN
A future tale of private detectives, AIs, Nanobots, love and death.
£7.99 (+ £1.50 UK p&p) Standard p/b ISBN: 1-903889-65-0

BREATHE by CHRISTOPHER FOWLER
The Office meets *Night of the Living Dead.*
£7.99 (+ £1.50 UK p&p) Standard p/b ISBN: 1-903889-67-7
£25.00 (+ £1.50 UK p&p) Deluxe h/b ISBN: 1-903889-68-5

HOUDINI'S LAST ILLUSION by STEVE SAVILE
Can the master illusionist Harry Houdini outwit the dead shades of his past?
£7.99 (+ £1.50 UK p&p) Standard p/b ISBN: 1-903889-66-9

ALICE'S JOURNEY BEYOND THE MOON by R J CARTER
A sequel to the classic Lewis Carroll tales.
£6.99 (+ £1.50 UK p&p) Standard p/b ISBN: 1-903889-76-6
£30.00 (+ £1.50 UK p&p) Deluxe h/b ISBN: 1-903889-77-4

APPROACHING OMEGA by ERIC BROWN
A colonisation mission to Earth runs into problems.
£7.99 (+ £1.50 UK p&p) Standard p/b ISBN: 1-903889-98-7
£30.00 (+ £1.50 UK p&p) Deluxe h/b ISBN: 1-903889-99-5

VALLEY OF LIGHTS by STEPHEN GALLAGHER
A cop comes up against a body-hopping murderer …
£9.99 (+ £2.50 UK p&p) Standard p/b ISBN: 1-903889-74-X
£30.00 (+ £2.50 UK p&p) Deluxe h/b ISBN: 1-903889-75-8

PARISH DAMNED by LEE THOMAS
Vampires attack an American fishing town.
£7.99 (+ £1.50 UK p&p) Standard p/b ISBN: 1-84583-040-7

MORE THAN LIFE ITSELF by JOE NASSISE
What would you do to save the life of someone you love?
£7.99 (+ £1.50 UK p&p) Standard p/b ISBN: 1-84583-042-3

PRETTY YOUNG THINGS by DOMINIC MCDONAGH
A nest of lesbian rave bunny vampires is at large in Manchester. When Chelsey's ex-boyfriend is taken as food, Chelsey has to get out fast.
£7.99 (+ £1.50 UK p&p) Standard p/b ISBN: 1-84583-045-8

A MANHATTAN GHOST STORY by T M WRIGHT
Do you see ghosts? A classic tale of love and the supernatural.
£9.99 (+ £2.50 UK p&p) Standard p/b ISBN: 1-84583-048-2

SHROUDED BY DARKNESS: TALES OF TERROR edited by ALISON L R DAVIES
An anthology of tales guaranteed to bring a chill to the spine. This collection has been published to raise money for DebRA, a national charity working on behalf of people with the genetic skin blistering condition, Epidermolysis Bullosa (EB). Featuring stories by: Debbie Bennett, Poppy Z Brite, Simon Clark, Storm Constantine, Peter Crowther, Alison L R Davies, Paul Finch, Christopher Fowler, Neil Gaiman, Gary Greenwood, David J Howe, Dawn Knox, Tim Lebbon, Charles de Lint, Steven Lockley & Paul Lewis, James Lovegrove, Graham Masterton, Richard Christian Matheson, Justina Robson, Mark Samuels, Darren Shan and Michael Marshall Smith. With a frontispiece by Clive Barker and a foreword by Stephen Jones. Deluxe hardback cover by Simon Marsden.
£12.99 (+ £2.50 UK p&p) Standard p/b ISBN: 1-84583-046-6
£50.00 (+ £2.50 UK p&p) Deluxe h/b ISBN: 978-1-84583-047-2

BLACK TIDE by DEL STONE JR
A college professor and his students find themselves trapped by an encroaching hoarde of zombies following a waste spillage.
£7.99 (+ £1.50 UK p&p) Standard p/b ISBN: 978-1-84583-043-4

TV/FILM GUIDES

DOCTOR WHO

THE TELEVISION COMPANION: THE UNOFFICIAL AND
UNAUTHORISED GUIDE TO DOCTOR WHO
by DAVID J HOWE & STEPHEN JAMES WALKER
Complete episode guide (1963 – 1996) to the popular TV show.
£14.99 (+ £4.75 UK p&p) Standard p/b ISBN: 1-903889-51-0

THE HANDBOOK: THE UNOFFICIAL AND UNAUTHORISED
GUIDE TO THE PRODUCTION OF DOCTOR WHO
by DAVID J HOWE, STEPHEN JAMES WALKER and MARK
STAMMERS
Complete guide to the making of *Doctor Who* (1963 – 1996).
£14.99 (+ £4.75 UK p&p) Standard p/b ISBN: 1-903889-59-6
£30.00 (+ £4.75 UK p&p) Deluxe h/b ISBN: 1-903889-96-0

BACK TO THE VORTEX: THE UNOFFICIAL AND
UNAUTHORISED GUIDE TO DOCTOR WHO 2005 by J SHAUN
LYON
Complete guide to the 2005 series of *Doctor Who* starring
Christopher Eccleston as the Doctor
£12.99 (+ £2.50 UK p&p) Standard p/b ISBN: 1-903889-78-2
£30.00 (+ £2.50 UK p&p) Deluxe h/b ISBN: 1-903889-79-0

SECOND FLIGHT: THE UNOFFICIAL AND UNAUTHORISED
GUIDE TO DOCTOR WHO 2006 by J SHAUN LYON
Complete guide to the 2006 series of *Doctor Who*, starring David
Tennant as the Doctor
£12.99 (+ £2.50 UK p&p) Standard p/b ISBN: 1-84583-008-3
£30.00 (+ £2.50 UK p&p) Deluxe h/b ISBN: 1-84583-009-1

WHOGRAPHS: THEMED AUTOGRAPH BOOK
80 page autograph book with an SF theme
£4.50 (+ £1.50 UK p&p) Standard p/b ISBN: 1-84583-110-1

TALKBACK: THE UNOFFICIAL AND UNAUTHORISED DOCTOR WHO INTERVIEW BOOK: VOLUME 1: THE SIXTIES edited by STEPHEN JAMES WALKER
Interviews with cast and behind the scenes crew who worked on *Doctor Who* in the sixties
£12.99 (+ £2.50 UK p&p) Standard p/b ISBN: 1-84583-006-7
£30.00 (+ £2.50 UK p&p) Deluxe h/b ISBN: 1-84583-007-5

TALKBACK: THE UNOFFICIAL AND UNAUTHORISED DOCTOR WHO INTERVIEW BOOK: VOLUME 2: THE SEVENTIES edited by STEPHEN JAMES WALKER
Interviews with cast and behind the scenes crew who worked on *Doctor Who* in the seventies
£12.99 (+ £2.50 UK p&p) Standard p/b ISBN: 1-84583-010-5
£30.00 (+ £2.50 UK p&p) Deluxe h/b ISBN: 1-84583-011-3

TALKBACK: THE UNOFFICIAL AND UNAUTHORISED DOCTOR WHO INTERVIEW BOOK: VOLUME 3: THE EIGHTIES edited by STEPHEN JAMES WALKER
Interviews with cast and behind the scenes crew who worked on *Doctor Who* in the eighties
£12.99 (+ £2.50 UK p&p) Standard p/b ISBN: 978-1-84583-014-4
£30.00 (+ £2.50 UK p&p) Deluxe h/b ISBN: 978-1-84583-015-1

HOWE'S TRANSCENDENTAL TOYBOX: SECOND EDITION by DAVID J HOWE & ARNOLD T BLUMBERG
Complete guide to *Doctor Who* Merchandise 1963–2002.
£25.00 (+ £4.75 UK p&p) Standard p/b ISBN: 1-903889-56-1

HOWE'S TRANSCENDENTAL TOYBOX: UPDATE No 1: 2003 by DAVID J HOWE & ARNOLD T BLUMBERG
Complete guide to *Doctor Who* Merchandise released in 2003.
£7.99 (+ £1.50 UK p&p) Standard p/b ISBN: 1-903889-57-X

HOWE'S TRANSCENDENTAL TOYBOX: UPDATE No 2: 2004-2005 by DAVID J HOWE & ARNOLD T BLUMBERG
Complete guide to *Doctor Who* Merchandise released in 2004 and 2005.
£7.99 (+ £1.50 UK p&p) Standard p/b ISBN: 1-84583-012-1

TORCHWOOD

INSIDE THE HUB: THE UNOFFICIAL AND UNAUTHORISED GUIDE TO TORCHWOOD by STEPHEN JAMES WALKER
Complete guide to the 2006 series of *Torchwood*, starring John Barrowman as Captain Jack Harkness
£12.99 (+ £2.50 UK p&p) Standard p/b ISBN: 978-1-84583-013-7

BLAKE'S 7

LIBERATION: THE UNOFFICIAL AND UNAUTHORISED GUIDE TO BLAKE'S 7 by ALAN STEVENS & FIONA MOORE
Complete episode guide to the popular TV show.
Featuring a foreword by David Maloney
£12.99 (+ £2.50 UK p&p) Standard p/b ISBN: 1-903889-54-5

SURVIVORS

THE END OF THE WORLD?: THE UNOFFICIAL AND UNAUTHORISED GUIDE TO SURVIVORS by ANDY PRIESTNER & RICH CROSS
Complete guide to Terry Nation's *Survivors*
£12.99 (+ £2.50 UK p&p) Standard p/b ISBN: 1-84583-001-6

CHARMED

TRIQUETRA: THE UNOFFICIAL AND UNAUTHORISED GUIDE TO CHARMED by KEITH TOPPING
Complete guide to *Charmed*
£12.99 (+ £2.50 UK p&p) Standard p/b ISBN: 1-84583-002-4

24

A DAY IN THE LIFE: THE UNOFFICIAL AND UNAUTHORISED GUIDE TO 24 by KEITH TOPPING
Complete episode guide to the first season of the popular TV show.
£9.99 (+ £2.50 p&p) Standard p/b ISBN: 1-903889-53-7

FILMS

A VAULT OF HORROR by KEITH TOPPING
A guide to 80 classic (and not so classic) British Horror Films.
£12.99 (+ £4.75 UK p&p) Standard p/b ISBN: 1-903889-58-8

BEAUTIFUL MONSTERS: THE UNOFFICIAL AND
UNAUTHORISED GUIDE TO THE ALIEN AND PREDATOR
FILMS by DAVID McINTEE
A guide to the Alien and Predator Films.
£9.99 (+ £2.50 UK p&p) Standard p/b ISBN: 1-903889-94-4

ZOMBIEMANIA: 80 FILMS TO DIE FOR by DR ARNOLD T
BLUMBERG & ANDREW HERSHBERGER
A guide to 80 classic zombie films, along with an extensive
filmography of over 500 additional titles
£12.99 (+ £2.50 UK p&p) Standard p/b ISBN: 1-84583-003-2

CRIME

THE LONG, BIG KISS GOODBYE by SCOTT MONTGOMERY
Hardboiled thrills as Jack Sharp gets involved with a dame called Kitty.
£7.99 (+ £1.50 UK p&p) Standard p/b ISBN: 978-1-84583-109-7

MIKE RIPLEY

The first three titles in Mike Ripley's acclaimed 'Angel' series of comic crime novels.

JUST ANOTHER ANGEL by MIKE RIPLEY
£9.99 (+ £1.50 UK p&p) Standard p/b ISBN: 1-84583-106-3
ANGEL TOUCH by MIKE RIPLEY
£9.99 (+ £1.50 UK p&p) Standard p/b ISBN: 1-84583-107-1
ANGEL HUNT by MIKE RIPLEY
£9.99 (+ £1.50 UK p&p) Standard p/b ISBN: 1-84583-108-X

HANK JANSON

Classic pulp crime thrillers from the 1940s and 1950s.

TORMENT by HANK JANSON
£9.99 (+ £1.50 UK p&p) Standard p/b ISBN: 1-903889-80-4
WOMEN HATE TILL DEATH by HANK JANSON
£9.99 (+ £1.50 UK p&p) Standard p/b ISBN: 1-903889-81-2
SOME LOOK BETTER DEAD by HANK JANSON
£9.99 (+ £1.50 UK p&p) Standard p/b ISBN: 1-903889-82-0
SKIRTS BRING ME SORROW by HANK JANSON
£9.99 (+ £1.50 UK p&p) Standard p/b ISBN: 1-903889-83-9
WHEN DAMES GET TOUGH by HANK JANSON
£9.99 (+ £1.50 UK p&p) Standard p/b ISBN: 1-903889-85-5
ACCUSED by HANK JANSON
£9.99 (+ £1.50 UK p&p) Standard p/b ISBN: 1-903889-86-3

KILLER by HANK JANSON
£9.99 (+ £1.50 UK p&p) Standard p/b ISBN: 1-903889-87-1
FRAILS CAN BE SO TOUGH by HANK JANSON
£9.99 (+ £1.50 UK p&p) Standard p/b ISBN: 1-903889-88-X
BROADS DON'T SCARE EASY by HANK JANSON
£9.99 (+ £1.50 UK p&p) Standard p/b ISBN: 1-903889-89-8
KILL HER IF YOU CAN by HANK JANSON
£9.99 (+ £1.50 UK p&p) Standard p/b ISBN: 1-903889-90-1
LILIES FOR MY LOVELY by HANK JANSON
£9.99 (+ £1.50 UK p&p) Standard p/b ISBN: 1-903889-91-X
BLONDE ON THE SPOT by HANK JANSON
£9.99 (+ £1.50 UK p&p) Standard p/b ISBN: 1-903889-92-8

Non-fiction

THE TRIALS OF HANK JANSON by STEVE HOLLAND
£12.99 (+ £2.50 UK p&p) Standard p/b ISBN: 1-903889-84-7

TELOS PUBLISHING
c/o Beech House, Chapel Lane, Moulton, Cheshire, CW9
8PQ, England
Email: orders@telos.co.uk
Web: www.telos.co.uk

To order copies of any Telos books, please visit our website where there are full details of all titles and facilities for worldwide credit card online ordering, or send a cheque or postal order (UK only) for the appropriate amount (including postage and packing – note that four or more titles are post free in the UK), together with details of the book(s) you require, plus your name and address to the above address. Overseas readers please send two international reply coupons for details of prices and postage rates.